Radiant Publishing House Inc.
P.O. Box 379
Walden, NY 12586
www.radiantpublishinghouse.com

Paperback 2nd Edition

ISBN: 978-0-9991857-4-2

For Carl, Doreen, and Nicole; who taught me how to read, write, and comprehend in both literature and life.

Index

All bolded words may be found with further definition
in the Tome of Insights on page 213.

M.C. Grimm

RADIANT HEROES

Episode 1: A Fantastic Youth

M.C. Grimm

I

<u>The Cleric of Tristian</u>

*"Let it by the deeds we practice in which our character
be judged."*
The Generous Life – A Tribute of Mora.

Mantis Lane had divided the city of **Tristian** since the day it was founded. To the north was **Premier**, the stone and marble estates of the nobles. To the south was the **Commons**, the wooden shacks of the less fortunate. This clear division was primarily due to Mantis Lane having held many central and more limited services. Building number 27 was one of these more frequented establishments. It was marked by a series of smeared healing sigils on the windows, obscuring an assortment of potions displayed on the shelves. The writing on the window was illegible, but everyone in town knew this was the home and office of Lavi Cheng, the town **cleric** and healer.

Lavi and his young son, Lee, were the only healers of skill in Tristian and were available at every hour of the day. They both were of **human** descent and were gifted in the rare magical art of healing. Throughout the entire **Radiant Empire,** their skills would be an in demand. For Tristian in particular, they were invaluable.

Lavi was going through his routine of arranging the herbs and straightening the gurneys when they heard the small bell at the front of the shop tinkling and the thud of the double-front doors crashing into the wall. Lavi raced down the hall from the storeroom in haste. He angled into the bedroom as he passed and leaned in with a smack of his shirt, "Up, boy!"

Lee obediently rolled from bed and began fumbling into his robes. He knew he was not moving fast enough, as Lavi kept whipping at him with pieces of his wardrobe.

"Move like it was *your* life at stake!" Lavi scolded.

They moved quickly out of the bedroom, into the main treatment center, and rushed into the lobby. In front of the open doors were two **dwarven** men limply supporting a third. The third man had a crossbow bolt protruding from his eye, blood dripping down his face. Even from across the room, Lee could smell the rank scent of cheap ale.

"Please, we need help, our friend's been shot-dead!" The red-haired dwarf shouted, lifting his unconscious comrade.

Lavi sighed, waved them into the treatment center, and pointed to one of the gurneys, "There." His eyes scanned up and down the dwarf - as if he was oblivious to the bolt stuck in his eye, but intently read his energy.

The blonde dwarf stomped his foot, "Well, aren't you going to do something? The bolt is here in his eye. It is over here." He continuously gestured to it, as if Lavi couldn't see where it was.

"There are some matters we must first discuss. Firstly, welcome to Lavi's Clinic. Normally I would ask *what ails you*, but the problem is quite clear. Next, the payment of 15 gold pieces?" Lavi held out his hand patiently until his palm was met with a coin purse. He placed it on the counter behind him. "Excellent." His eyes scrolled over his patient. "Thank you. Secondly, what exactly happened?"

The blonde dwarf attempted to explain what had happened, but he was choked with emotion. The other put a hand on his shoulder to silence him. "It's alright, I'll tell him. We were tracking some **orcs** that had raided one of our caravans' days ago. We were on their trail and followed them into the wood. See, we caught up to them, and were showing them the wrath of our hammers, when one of them tried to make a run for it. My clan-brother here took a shot with his crossbow, but stumbled and hit poor Nor in the eye."

Looking intently at Nor, Lavi asked, "The wood you are speaking of, East Tristian Wood?"

"West," Sobbed the blonde dwarf.

"The West Tristian Wood is about a four-hour hike from here, perhaps six-hours to carry Nor as well, and yet this man has been dead for close to twenty-two hours." Lavi was moving around the table, analyzing the body. "What exactly did you do with the rest of that time that was more important than saving your friend?" He asked with a chuckle.

The red-haired dwarf did not speak for a moment, he was staring down at Nor. His eyes gleamed until he blinked once, deliberately, to release the swimming tears down his face.

The blonde dwarf spoke, "It was my fault. I knew he was dead, but I also knew we had time for you to, you know—work your magic. I didn't think he was in real danger, so I left him back at the inn, stopped by the tavern and found myself some–" his eyes fell on Lee as if ashamed, "some *company*. I didn't think he was dead-dead. And now, I just don't know."

Lavi smiled warmly and didn't seem bothered at the dwarf's emotion, "And yet, you *both* reek of ale?"

"I thought my brother was going to bring him so I too left him at the inn and went to stock up on supplies." The red-haired dwarf said, "Then...I went to a couple of taverns to have a few myself and by luck, stumbled across him. It was then I thought that Nor might be in worse shape than we originally thought, so we brought him here straight away. He's been starting to smell."

Lavi had already began shifting around the room grabbing at vials from the shelves. He collected some that were labeled **phoenix dust**, **dried cocoon silk**, and **sky sparks**. He then grabbed a handful of dried **heartbane** from the clothesline overhead and placed them all together on a surgical cart. He began crushing them and mixing them together in a mortar and pestle. Periodically, he waved his hand over it to illuminate a warm green light. "Luckily," he said as a spark shot from the bowl, "I am familiar with resurrection rituals. For the extra charge of 15 gold pieces, I can bring him back and still tend to his eye. Since he has not yet been dead for twenty-four hours, it will most definitely work."

The blonde dwarf jerked a coin purse from his belt and held it out to Lavi. Lavi shook his head as he was focused on his patient, and gestured towards Lee. With his father's nod, Lee snatched the purse and tucked it into his robe.

Lavi stopped mixing and silently held his hands over the bowl. A low resounding hum began emanating throughout the room, accompanied by a soft static sound. He lifted his hands and surprisingly, it appeared nearly empty. A single item remained at the bottom. Lavi extended two fingers and delicately picked up a small, shiny, brown seed that was no larger than a single peanut. Everyone stood silent in confusion until Lavi said softly, "The **seed of life**. The seed was first in creation and it became the flower, the fruit, and brought life. It was not the first of attempts. No, many seeds before it were sown. Unfortunately, at that time, conditions weren't yet right for life to grow."

Lee excitedly interrupted, "Not until the maker separated the realms to allow for different life to bloom across the land and sea or sky—even creatures from the **void** were seeds planted to grow within the darkness."

Lavi slowly turned to Lee, his eyes hardened, and jaw clenched. "Yes, well." He tilted back Nor's head and placed the small seed in his mouth. While rubbing at his throat, Lavi gently rested his ear near the mouth to listen. Suddenly, he felt a soft breath on his cheek. It was a fragile, single breath. He stood up and watched as Nor's chest began to rise and fall regularly, becoming more stable, more rhythmic. "I think it would be nice if he woke up with both eyes. Lee, grab my elixir."

Lee did not move. He was entranced at watching the blush of color flow back to the dwarf's face. The pulse in his neck showed that his heartbeat was hastening. Lee wondered if it was the surging magic of the seed, or if his heart was making up for missed beats.

"I said now, boy!" Lavi scolded.

He obeyed, "I'm sorry."

Lavi was holding the bolt in one hand and held out the other to snatch the illuminating elixir from Lee. He removed the cork with his teeth and quickly downed the elixir for himself. He quivered with a chill and seemed to be revitalized by it. In a quick motion, he yanked up the bolt squirting a quick shot of blood across his face. Bits of meat and stringy vessels dangled from the bolt as he handed it to Lee. "Discard this, boy." He held both hands over Nor's face, emitting that same soft green glow. Lavi was still and focused, sweat forming on his brow. When he finally moved away, there now was a smooth tan eyelid, gently resting over the bulge of a dwarven eye.

The red-haired dwarf was staring at Lavi in amazement, grabbing at the wall to hold himself up. "That was amazing, you really did it." They were both in tears. "The cleric did it, he saved him."

"He will need a couple of days to fully recover. I would like you to leave him here so my son can look after him." Lavi looked at Lee, "Be sure to keep him hydrated and in bed."

"Of course," the red-haired dwarf recomposed himself and pulled close his brother, "We will be back in a few days to collect him. Thank you, Lavi. Truly, there are no words to show what you've done for us. You brought our brother back to us." Then, still with a look of disbelief and awe, they left the building.

Lee was staring at Nor with a smile, studying him and his rejuvenated eye. "He *is* stable father; he may be ready tomorrow." He had turned to face his father with excitement and was greeted with a forceful smack across his face that knocked him onto his back.

"Do not interrupt me when I am speaking with a patient." Lavi spoke with authority. "And, do not snatch gold from clients like some beggar. We are a business and *will* remain professional at all times."

Lee's tongue had a taste of iron as his split lip bled into his mouth, "Yes father, I was wrong to do those things. It won't happen again."

Lavi wore a look of disgust, "Yes, and you would do well to act quickly when I ask you to do something. Only have me ask things of you a single time. These are people we are saving, and I can't be repeating myself, do you understand?"

Lee waved his green glowing hand over his face. The blood stopped dripping from his lip. "I understand, father." He spoke without emotion, "I will listen more carefully and act more quickly."

"Yes, you will." Lavi redirected his stare around the stocks of herbs on the shelves. "I must not have noticed how much of the heartbane we've been going through. Go to the south market and get a tote of it. Take one gold piece from the dwarf's payment and leave the rest on my desk."

Lee did not speak. He did just as he was told and left without a moment of hesitation. On his way out of the door, there was another patient coming in—an elf holding a couple of his own severed fingers. Lee felt relief knowing that his father would be busy for a while and wouldn't notice how long he might be gone. He could even pass by **Gardener Park** and not get in trouble for having fun.

Lee traveled only a few blocks north when he decided to take advantage of the moment and go down Gardener Road – his favorite street. It was lined with well-trimmed shrubs and bushes, alive with colorful flowers and sweet scents. Here grew many flowers that someone as educated to healing arts as Lee could quickly identify. Helpful remedies like **ostrich blossom**, with its vibrant purple petals that, when boiled, could cure warts and pimples. There was also the yellow and orange decorated **tigertail** that could be crushed into a fine wet residue and applied to small wounds for a seemingly instant heal. It was also excellent at preventing infection to fresh wounds, but was less commonly known. To most, these were just sweet scents. To Lee, they were more beautiful in other ways.

The succulent scents were enough to make the walk worthwhile, but Gardener Park had a set of swings with many slides and ladders that he especially enjoyed. Lee hesitated for a moment, and only a moment, to think of how upset his father would be if he were caught. Still, he ran out with a giddy excitement to swing across the monkey bars like an acrobat. There were only a couple of very small children there today with nannies, so he was free to jump on the slide and complete some back and forth over hurdles. Lee couldn't resist one last visit to the swings. He kicked higher and higher and finally, caught up in the sheer magic of the moment, let go and took flight spreading out his arms wide. He was hoping to fly away from this place, but too suddenly, reality hit him in the form of loose dirt and rock.

At the same time, a jingling thud met the ground next to him. A few loose coins from the dwarven coin purse sprawled out from beneath his now soiled robes.

"Oh no!" Lee said to himself as panic filled his thoughts. In his haste to be away from his father, he had only left one of the dwarven pouches behind. His eyes widened; would his father notice or could he put it away without being caught? All the thoughts of beatings and scolding rushed through his mind. No, he couldn't let this slow him down; he still had to stop at the market and finish his errand. He climbed to his feet, brushed off his robes, and made a dash towards the north market.

The northern market was known as Premier. It was a well-decorated and prestigious place filled with the most cultured vendors. Here, there were wine connoisseurs at their carts filled with beautiful bottles of ruby red wines, clothing carts with fancy silken robes, magical imbued weapon forges, and stalls with any raw material or herb that Lee could ever have need of. He slipped through the crowd of nobles and over to **Harryman's Herb**– a vendor of quality herbs. The door was held open by a large wooden barrel labeled, **Eel Wheat**.

Lee walked in, already placing his order without even noticing who was there, "Lester, I am in need of heartbane." Looking up, he realized there was a woman being helped ahead of him. "My apologies, I didn't mean to be rude."

Lester was a tall human with a baldhead that was always irregularly shiny. He also had the warmest smile, but without showing any teeth. "Oh, my dear boy, not at all, it is always good to see the young Master Cheng. It has been quite some time since I've seen you or your father. I've heard he's been shopping south in the Commons, not that I mind, of course. Anyway, I'm sure your need is greater than most, being as fine a cleric as yourself." Lester had finished with the woman and turned to reach for some heartbane from a shelf behind him. He started wrapping it in twine, "Can't be a cleric without heartbane now can you?"

Lee was relieved. "My father thought we had some in our cellar, but some mice had nested in it." He picked up the twined bunch. "How much for a tote worth?"

"That'll be one and five for a tote," Lester responded. He continued to wrap up his remaining stocks of heartbane, but paused as if remembering something. "Oh, young cleric, I had meant to ask if you had any insight on those animal attacks in the north village – if they are animal attacks? Has your clinic taken in any wounded?"

Lee quickly sifted through the pouch for one gold and five silver pieces. He spread them in his palm and handed them to Lester. "There has been no one to treat," he said. "My father says it would be cruel to resurrect one of these victims when they're not in one piece. He said something about how people linger in their moment of death and can relive it over-and-over again when it's as vicious as this is. I'm sorry, I talk too much." He laughed, but in his heart, he knew he was going to be late and in a lot of trouble. "I need to go, but I will let you know if I come across anything. Thank you again, Lester."

Lester waved, "Of course, Master Cheng. Be well, say hello to your father and do be sure to visit me soon."

Before these words had reached him, Lee had already turned and raced through the door and begun to sprint through the streets of Premier. He ran frantically as if his life was in jeopardy, and with his father, it very well could be. There was no chance that Lavi would believe he forgot to leave the pouch. Moreover, Lee knew there was no chance he would get away without a lashing.

Pushing through his fear, Lee arrived back at 27 Mantis Lane in record time. He attempted to peer through the stains and sigils but was only able to catch glimpses of movement between the smears. It looked like his father was sifting for tools near a procedural table. With a deep and anxious breath, Lee stepped inside.

His father was still tending to the elf that now had three of his four severed fingers re-attached. Lee felt a smile grow across his face, but as soon as his eyes met Lavi's, he was greeted with a scornful stare.

"Boy!" Lavi rushed towards Lee, "I have been waiting for this heartbane. What have you been doing? You should have rushed back."

Lee breathed a sigh of relief knowing the coin purse hadn't been noticed. He quickly handed over the heartbane and with a gentle tone said, "I am sorry father, Lester had to wait for his delivery man to drop off a crate."

Strangely, Lee's response made Lavi's face flush red. Lee could see the familiar vein in his neck pulsing furiously as if it was to burst. "Go to your room and get out of my face, I'll deal with you later."

He didn't waste a second to escape. With a stealthy maneuver, he was able to slide the coin purse onto the desk without it making a jingle. Lee shut the door behind him and threw himself onto his bed to curl up with his pillow. From underneath, he pulled out a brown leather-bound journal inscribed with a large imprint of a leafy tree. It was nearly full and bursting with loose sheets of sketch papers. Some of the artwork was simply shaded while others were colorful from his homemade pastels.

Lee opened to a fresh page and began to sketch. He was blurring the lines to show the speed of his legs pumping on the swings. Then, he began shading in all the petals of the tigertails and ostrich blossoms that were scattered around Gardener Park. He was about an hour invested before he heard the final goodbyes from the lobby and the chime of the door signaling the elf had left.

There was a series of rapid footsteps moving across the floor until they finally met the bedroom door with a force. Lavi entered, already boiling with anger, and crossed the room in what seemed like a single step. He grabbed Lee by his collar and with the back of his hand, smacked him across the face knocking him to the floor.

Lee immediately began to sob, "Father, please stop!" He held his hand up to his eye and felt a slow swelling, "what did I do?"

His hand was quickly swatted away, and Lavi was already on him, grabbing both sides of his collar, "*Why* did you go to Lester?"

Lee was confused, he was certain his father had discovered the missing pouch. "Lester? What does–"

Lavi shook him hard, slamming his back against the wall. "Lester is at Premier, I told you to take a single gold piece and go to the *south* market. Lester would charge at least one and five, so how did you pay for the rest? Have you been pocketing extra coin, boy?" He shook Lee again, "Have you?"

His head was spinning, and his vision was blurry, but Lee was able to piece it all together. His father hadn't noticed the coin purse gone, at all. Lee had gone to the wrong market by mistake and told Lavi about Lester when he first walked in. He made this happen to himself and he was smart enough to realize he would have to commit to this.

"Father," he started calmly with tears swimming in his eyes, "the last time I had gone to Lester, we had some credit there from eel wheat sold us that was already browning, remember? I was able to get the heartbane for the same price with the credit, but since it's from Lester, it's better quality."

Lavi narrowed his gaze, "I don't remember that. Why didn't you say something when you left?"

"Really," Lee said frantically, "you can go ask him. I just didn't want us to lose the credit. I didn't remember until I was already down the street and I knew I had to hurry back."

Lavi loosened his grip and stood. "Lee, just do as you are told. You are twelve years old. Thinking for yourself is dangerous. *I* know what is best and even though you were looking out for the business, you disobeyed me, boy. I hope you have learned your lesson." He then walked out of the room and slammed the door behind him.

Lee sat on the floor, holding his palms against his eyes, and loosening his hand from time to time to let the tears roll away. He hated being dishonest, but another beating today would've been too much for him.

It took him a few minutes to calm himself and regain his balance before picking up all the sketches that were thrown from his book in the scuffle. The edge of one familiar picture was sticking out from the others and Lee picked it up slowly. The paper was crinkled from being frequently handled and the pastels were runny. He held the sketch of vibrant colors that had shown a Lee from years ago—holding up a **cattletail rose** to an attractive, glowing young woman. She was holding him up in the air with her eyes closed, and the most joyous smile brightening her face. Lee stared at it and squeezed it to his chest, "I miss you so much, Mom. You would keep me safe."

And while Lee drifted off to sleep with only the pleasant memories of tenderness in his heart, little did he imagine; only unforgettable nightmares were to visit him that night.

II

Man and Monster

"There would be no feats of bravery without bouts of madness."
The Chill of Death – A Tribute to Crowlastte

Lee held the picture close as his tears wet the pastels. So tightly that they left a smear onto his robes. Before long, he sobbed himself into exhaustion and fell asleep curled atop his covers. He wasn't sure how long he was asleep, but the faint creak of the door woke him to observe his father enter and move to his own bed on the far side of the room. Lee watched for a moment as his father folded down the sheets and hesitated. He had turned to stare over at Lee and shook his head slow with disapproval. With a twisting gut, he held his breath to keep from sobbing. He kept his eyes tight, feeling a twisting ache in his chest, and fell back asleep.

It must have been around three in the morning when a thunderous banging began. The front door had nearly been pounded off the hinges as an articulate voice carried through, "Hello, Cleric Cheng! We are in need of your help. Please let us in. We apologize for the late hour, but please?"

Lavi leapt to his feet and was quickly dressing himself. "Boy, get your clothes on."

Lee instinctively got up, still dressed in his smeared robes from the day prior. For the first time, he had made it to the door before his father and slid the lock open, "Lavi's Clinic, what is your emergency?"

Outside the door stood three figures, all seemingly calm, unusual to the typical urgency that would knock in the middle of the night. The first was a tall human with green eyes and well-manicured blonde hair. He wore an elaborate blue and orange trimmed mages gown and stood with a poised smile that radiated charisma and confidence. The second man was in tattered black robes with pasty skin, messy white hair across his face, and painted with ornate tattoos – the marks of a **kai**. Every visible inch of him was marked with scars showing, at least what Lee could decipher— a deliberate procedure or even torture. The third figure was hanging limply over the scarred man's shoulder. His legs were twisting weakly as he attempted to reposition his feet and stand, albeit, unsuccessfully. He was partially shrouded in a dark cloak, but Lee could see lizard-like skin that was a flushed green color.

Lee froze for a moment before stepping aside to allow them into the procedural room. Lavi was already prepped and in front of a cot, pulling up a cart of routine tigertail and **cotton wheat** ointments. "Good evening gentlemen, I am Lavi Cheng and you have already met my son, Lee. What ails you?"

The smiling, green-eyed human led them over to the cot and heaved his **reptilian** friend up. He never lost his smirk and his hair stayed perfectly in place, as if held by magic. "We are terribly sorry to disturb you at this late hour, but our friend is in need of your skills. I am Tholden Moonstorm, this is Stein, and our wounded friend here is Grekk. We have coin for your treatment—with extra, for your discretion." He put his hand in his pocket and jingled coins as enticement.

Lavi removed the reptilian's cloak and then scanned him up and down. He waved his hands over him, emitting a soft green glow, which was slowly drawn to his chest. The lizard squirmed, forcing Tholden and Stein to quickly grab hold of his shoulders and pin him to the table. Lavi then tore open the shirt to show the flush scales of his chest, covered by a series of claw marks from his collar to his abdomen. Upon Lavi's closer inspection, the wounds appeared as if they were originally much deeper but had partially mended. The dried blood still on his scales showed that this happened very recently and could not possibly be naturally healed.

"How did you treat his wounds?"Lavi asked.

"We attempted to give him a healing potion," replied Tholden, "but, he kept vomiting it up."

"Interesting—very interesting." Lavi continued, searching over Grekk, and leaning closer to peer into the wounds. "And, what attacked him?"

"*This* is the part that requires your discretion." Tholden reached into his pocket and placed an overstuffed coin purse on the table. "Fifty gold pieces?"

Lavi nodded and gestured to Lee to take the purse. Lee eagerly took it from Tholden and clumsily tipped it, allowing a few coins to fall out and clang against the wooden floor.

"Pick them up, boy." Lavi scolded. "I am growing tired of your mistakes." He turned back to his patients who were looking on, uncomfortably. "My apologies for the boy, he is not the most competent assistant."

There was a brief silence before Tholden spoke again, "Yes, well. As I was saying, what attacked him was a **vetaless**. We did manage to catch up to one of them, but only then did we learn what it even was. You see, we were sent on a quest from General Dart of the Empire to track down a creature that's been terrorizing the nearby areas." He narrowed one eye with a smolder."You may have heard of us; I recently conquered a hydra at **Sundale**. They are constructing a monument in their town square in my-" he caught himself, "I mean, *our* honor. Have you heard the tales?"

"No, I have not. I have heard of these attacks, however," Lavi said, "they were up in Premier and the **Northern Villas**. Did you manage to kill it?"

Stein's face was stern, "Not yet."

Tholden continued, "No, we were forced to come here. Even with *all* of my great strength and wisdom, I was not ready for something like this. We were not ready for the **corrupted**, no less the **vetala** itself. After Grekk was mauled, I knew we had to re-think our plan of attack, and find him help, of course."

"Of course." Lavi kept his focus on the patient. He waved his hands back and forth. There was a soft green glow from his very essence, radiating down over Grekk with a warm energy that seemed to flicker and periodically spark. After a few minutes, beads of sweat were dripping from Lavi's forehead. "This is proving to be a most powerful corruption. I fear the vetala you encounter may prove to be more than you are prepared for. Yes, I fear we may be dealing with a **vetala lord**." Lavi turned towards Lee, "Boy, bring me whatever phoenix dust we have."

Tholden stepped out of the way, as Lee rushed past. "Wait, you think that the creature we have come for is a vetala lord? What does that mean, exactly? All I know of vetala is that they turn lesser humans and creatures into their corrupted and that they burn from **radiant** magic. They are also shape shifters, so more than likely, his monstrous form won't look anything like his public face."

"A vetala lord or Alpha is an ancient being; it is no longer a simple creature of darkness. Assume it has consumed the life of countless mortals and has taken their power into its own. Stories would say that they no longer possess the dead but corrupt the living to obey as their minions and vessels. The curse of a vetala lord would be unbreakable, and his power would be most terrifying. I do not envy your group." He concentrated for a moment and then continued, "I suppose it could be described as being similar to a **djinn** or a **vampire**, if one was to speak more plainly."

Tholden tapped his foot. "So, sever the head or pierce the heart?"

"Similar as vetala – or vetaless are, they aren't the same as those other creatures. No, they are much more formidable, if you believe the stories. I've heard you could kill them more conventionally, as they are normally possessing cadavers." Lavi peered over at their pale faces. "Cadavers are corpses. You know the vetala would reanimate a dead body and force its own spirit into it? Regardless, to kill a lord would mean it has reached its most frightening form—that would be where the stories have met a gruesome end."

"How certain of you are this?" Tholden asked.

Lavi scoffed, "Not at all certain. I studied the curse to treat it, killing the creature was never my concern."

Lee ran back into the room, catching Tholden without a grin for the first time. He quickly moved towards Lavi when he accidently bumped the surgical cart and toppled the tigertail petals to the floor. He looked up into the furious eyes of his father.

"I'm sor-" his voice was cut short by the landing of an open palm on his cheek.

"Enough of your stupidity, you worthless child!" Lavi was now beaming red with frustration and already dripping with sweat. He took a deep breath and turned to face his clients but was stopped by a wall of muscle. Stein must have moved towards him while he was dealing with Lee.

"Do not touch him again," Stein said, sternly.

"With all due respect, I will discipline my son as I see fit." Lavi maneuvered past the immobile Stein and continued preparing several vials or elixir.

"My humblest apologies for my friend here, he is quite partial to children," Tholden jittered with a nervous laugh. He quickly changed the subject, "What is it you are mixing there?"

Lavi had arranged nine of the vials on the cart beside him. "It is **shadowbane**, also known as **lights kiss** or **sun wisp**. It will protect you and your friends from becoming infected should you be slashed or bitten by the creatures."

"I see." Tholden investigated a vial of the liquid. "Remarkable. What will it do for Grekk?"

"He has not yet fed on human blood, correct?" Lavi questioned.

"Not at all," Tholden said.

"This will cure him so long as the infection was not from a vetala lord, which seems to be the case here," he replied.

Tholden hesitated. "And if it is a vetala lord, as is the likelihood?"

Lavi continued working and answered confidently, "If that's the case, then there is no cure and he will become corrupted. I would then be obligated to put him to rest."

Lee jumped forward, forgetting the lesson imparted from the pink handprint on his cheek, "We can't kill him! We swore to save lives and do no harm to the injured and sick."

"I am well aware of what oath I have taken, boy, but we can't allow infection to spread further through the city. We also must consider the rest of the population. Your mind is still too small to understand."

Lee pleaded, "No father, we would have to find another way. We can read through the lore and maybe find some past history on th-"

"Enough." Lavi landed a backhand across Lee's other cheek. "I do not need to explain everything to you. Shut your mouth, watch and learn, or you will find yourself out in the streets while I take on a new apprentice with some respect."

Lavi turned back to his patient, but Stein was now standing only a foot away. His eyes glowed and fixed onto Lavi with a malevolent stare. A powerful essence radiated from him that heated the room and distorted the air. The cloak on his back began to sway as if caught in a wind. "I told you *not* to touch him again."

"And *I* told *you*, I will discipline him as I see fit. Mind your tongue when you speak to me, I am a Master Cleric." Lavi said with contempt, not recognizing the peril he was in. "You *will* show me some respect."

Stein's damning stare shown in his judgment that Lavi held no remorse for the abuse he inflicted upon Lee. In a calculated rage, his pupils dilated, and his lip curled to the corner of his mouth. He had slid back his right foot and positioned his empty hands as if he was grasping something. Something heavy. Suddenly, as if the very light of the room itself warped in a flicker of blackness, a long gleaming shaft appeared in his hands. It reflected only a sinister darkness around it and resembled that of a scythe. At the head was a long crooked, crescent blade that had shown as an obsidian metal. It erupted into flame, casting a bright burst of light through the room. The heat was intense to everyone near him, but Stein didn't seem to notice it.

"What are you doing, Stein?" Tholden didn't move an inch. "Let's not doing anything hasty here."

Stein ignored Tholden, all of his attention focused on Lavi, "I will only show you the respect that you have given to this child."

In a flash, Stein took a single step forward. He arced the flaming blade and cut into Lavi with a deep slash from his neck to his navel. Blood erupted from Lavi's throat and splattered over Stein's unflinching face. The crimson speckled his white hair and showered across the room like rain. Lavi stumbled forward in an attempt to regain his footing, but frantically realized too late that he had fatally misjudged this strange man. He bumped into the table and rolled over Grekk to collapse on the floor. The blood sprayed from his neck. While he tossed about in his frenzy, he attempted to cover and heal it with his hands. However, he was too late and was already beginning to lose consciousness

From the table there were two deep audible sniffs. Tholden slowly turned his head towards Grekk, whose eyes had shot open—glossy and bloodshot. With inhuman speed, he twisted to a perched position on the bed, breathing and snarling like a crazed beast. His mouth was hanging open, exposing bone white fangs. He leapt towards Lavi, dodging Tholden's readied grasp. Grekk buried his teeth into Lavi, proceeding in his wicked indulgence with crunching noises as he tore through flesh and muscle to reach the bone.

Stein looked on with a mad grin and allowed his magical scythe to dissipate.

Tholden grabbed onto Grekk and began to wrestle him off Lavi. With great difficulty, he pulled him off and pinned him to the floor. Grekk continued biting and chomping now at Tholden. "Stein, I could use a hand."

"You have him," Stein replied. He turned and started towards Lee.

Lavi was now slumped in a corner, his chest cavity torn open to expose his ribs and a shredded artery. There was a chunk torn out of his neck and burns over his clothes from the flame of the scythe. Embers were smoking at the fabric. Lee looked at him in horror with a frozen, fearful stare. Tears streamed down his face and his entire body began to tremble, "Why, why did you kill my father?"

Stein crouched down, eye to eye with Lee, calming him with only the chill and charm of his stare. He spoke deliberately, "Lee, your father was—a monster. That's why he was so violent and abusive."

Lee wiped his tears away and looked back at Stein, confused, "What? He wasn't a monster, he was my father." He look back at the remnants of Lavi."He was human. What are you talking about?"

"A man can be a monster, Lee. Monsters hurt people, but a father is supposed to look out for his son. Does he look out for you or does he hurt you?"

"He hurts me," Lee sobbed, again, "but he does it because I make a lot of mistakes and he wants me to do better."

"You are young; you're supposed to make mistakes." Stein shook his head, "No, Lee. He was a man who became a monster. Not through disease or magic, but through bad choices. You never deserved to be treated that way and you never have to be again. You are free of him, before he could turn *you* into him. Or, do you think how he treated you was right? What are you Lee, a man or a monster?" He peered into him, "What do you want to be?"

He began to sob, the depth of this question drowning him beneath the grizzly nightmare he just witnessed, "I don't know what I am."

Suddenly, Grekk rolled over and lost consciousness. The fight with Tholden and Lavi had finally overcame him.

Tholden stepped off him and moved towards them. He crouched next to Stein, "Nonsense, you advocated not to kill Grekk. You stood up to your father and were willing to find another way to cure him. That makes you more of a man than most. If I do say so, myself."

Lee rubbed his eyes, "I just don't want anyone to die."

Stein nodded in agreement, "I understand how you feel. We can still use your help if you want to come with us. We don't have anyone with your healing skills."

"Are you sure that's a good idea?" Tholden interrupted.

Stein shot Tholden a stern look.

"You mean, help you stop monsters? Or help save people?" Lee asked.

"Stopping monsters saves people and if you're with us - I can keep you safe," Stein said, softly.

Lee's gaze fell to the floor. He then stared at the smeared pastels on his robes and tears swelled up in his eyes, "I haven't felt safe in so long. I want to help people. I can help."

Stein grasped him on both shoulders and focused his attention. "You will be okay. I will keep you safe and no one will treat you as he did ever again. Do you want to come with us?"

"I want to help people," Lee replied. His eyes fixed onto Lavi's corpse and sadness was churning into anger. He could feel the twist of emotions—from shock, to anger. He thought about how long he had been trapped in this place. His stare then followed a trail of blood that was running along a floorboard and into the closet. The closet that defined so many horrific memories of punishment. "Yes, I'll come. I can help."

Stein smiled, "Then go pack your things and we'll head back to camp."

Tholden looked on as Lee left the room. He turned to Stein, "Are you sure we should be bringing him along? We are going after a possible vetala lord and traveling with an infected reptilian. It's not really the safest environment for him."

"He's more capable than his father," Stein responded. "I can see that in his eyes, he has strong magic within him—pure light."

"Grekk needs him, I suppose. And, who knows what else we might encounter. You sure know how to recruit, Stein-baby." Tholden gave him a quick jab in the arm.

"Don't," he warned. "It's not like we are using him. We freed him."

Tholden's eyebrow nearly met his hairline. "Wait, you don't mean—you killed his father for beating him...that's it?"

"I killed him so that Lee wouldn't have to live his life as an abused servant."

"What do you care?" Tholden scoffed. "Never mind, you are one scary man, Stein. Now that I think about it, we shouldn't leave this building standing. No one should find the cleric like that. It would raise questions, maybe even an investigation."

"Whatever you think." Stein said.

"Of course," Tholden sighed. "You would rather kill every last guard in town than show some discretion. Don't worry, I'll take care of it."

It didn't take long for Lee to come out carrying two small duffle bags that dangled off the end of a wooden staff. "I have some of our stock and all the clothes I own. I'm ready."

"Good, I hope you actually have everything you need. Should we give this shadowbane to Grekk now?" Tholden asked, picking up all nine vials.

"Oh, yes, of course. We should all drink some. For Grekk, it will take a little while since he is already infected," Lee said. "For us, it will act as a protection."

They each forced down the elixir, gathered whatever herbs they could carry, and went out into the darkness of Mantis Lane. Standing in front of the clerical office, Lee looked back to the old sigils. He noticed now just how dusty and smeared they appeared on the glass. How did the place that brought so much good to the world become so worn down? Lee gave one last look at the grand wooden doors. For some reason, it appeared much smaller now, than ever before.

"I'm ready, Stein." he said with mild apprehension.

"Good." Stein crouched eye-level to Lee. "I know this is a lot to take in. I was treated terribly by my father too."

"You were?" Lee asked.

"In the most terrible ways you could ever imagine." He paused as if re-living horrific thoughts. "There is a darkness that lives inside some people. Lavi, your father, was filled with it but you – Lee, you are filled with light. If I didn't do what I did, someday that light would have been snuffed out. Like that of a candle, and you would be just as your father was. I couldn't let that happen. This group you are going to be a part of, they are ones who keep light alive. They are ones who find hope in the darkness and let the light inside you burn as bright as the sun itself."

"Did they save you from losing your light?" Lee asked with a soft tone, his eyes wide with hope.

His eyes searched up to the sky, "They are still working on it."

Lee smiled, "Well, I can help, too."

Stein began to walk down the street, supporting Grekk over his shoulder. Lee chased closely behind him, his duffle bags swaying on the end of his staff.

"How did you get those scars? Are they part of an initiation? How did you make that scythe appear? Is it magic?" Lee couldn't keep quiet now and wanted to know everything.

Stein smiled, "Let me answer, one at a time."

"Oh yeah, sorry. I talk too much." He hung his head.

"I don't think you talk too much at all."

"Really?" Lee asked with excitement.

"Really."

"Thanks."

"The scars are from fighting. I was trained from when I was even younger than you are to be a warrior and I've earned my fair share of cuts. The scythe is magic and I won it in what you could call a duel."

They were approaching what appeared to be stables in the south district when he heard a commotion coming from behind them. People were yelling, "Fire!" When he turned to investigate, he realized he must have been so caught up in his conversation with Stein that he didn't notice exactly where Tholden had disappeared to, but he could see thick black smoke bellowing up into the air where his home used to be.

He turned towards Stein with a quick jerk to ask and was met with a soft hand on his shoulder and a warm smile, "It will be okay, you're safe now. There are no monsters where we're going."

Lee wasn't sure why he trusted Stein, or even Tholden as much as he did, but he somehow felt safe for the first time in a long time. His shorter legs moved quickly to keep pace with Stein, "Where are we going?" he asked.

"It's just up ahead," said Stein.

"Who are these people?"

"Friends of ours."

"They're my friends, too?" asked Lee.

"You are with me, so yes. They are *our* friends."

"What if they don't like me?"

Stein looked him in the eyes without breaking pace, "Trust me, they are going to love you."

"What if they don't?" he replied.

Stein smiled, "Try to relax, it's not like they're going to eat you."

III

<u>Meeting the Family</u>

"The true source of strength is not in your sword, but in the courage to inspire the swords beside you."
The Wayward Warrior – A Tribute to Solihart.

Lee and his new comrades were now on the outermost part of the southern district. They were nearing a crooked barn, which was fading and peeling with the words *Ayla's Stable and Training Grounds*. It had no windows and, from here, appeared to have a double door that held strongly together through the years of neglect. The property's buildings appeared almost abandoned, except for a chatter coming from inside the barn. As they approached, Lee was able to see a small cottage tucked in the back of the lot and looking as decrepit as the rest. To his surprise, there was smoke dancing from the chimney. It seemed to blend into the clouds of the starlit sky. Stein narrowly slid open the barn door and led Lee and Grekk inside.

"We have a guest," Stein said while plopping Grekk to the ground.

Grekk seemed more energetic now. He perched himself up against the wall. "You could be a bit gentler with me," he said with a raspy and high-pitched voice, "I'm not at my best."

A deep voice bellowed from the other end of the barn, "what kind of guest?"

Lee hadn't notice the other figures in the corner until one stepped forward out of the dimness. The towering creature was walking slowly, straight towards him. There were two more shadowed figures lingering behind. Lee leaned back and awkwardly stared up at the creature. He was strapping and armored, with the face of a bull and broad horns to match. Lee tried to speak, but couldn't seem to find any words that made sense. It took him a few seconds more to finally yell, "You - have horns!"

Stein let out a soft chuckle which echoed from the others lurking in the corner of the barn.

To Lee's relief, the **minotaur** laughed boisterously, "Yes, I do. They're as old as I am, and twice as sharp."

"You mean half as dull, don't you?" asked the second man coming out of the shadow. He spoke in a hard accent, as if either **common tongue** was not his first language or that he was a bit dense. When his figure was more illuminated, Lee could see that this green skinned man. He had the lean build of a human with the complexion, jaw, and teeth of an orc. He was a **half-breed** of the two—human and orc.

"Care to find out what I meant?" the minotaur replied, turning to face him.

"Calm yourself, Marlow," the half-breed said dismissively. He knelt towards Lee and put out his hand, "Hello young scrap, my name is Garf of the Unkle Clan."

Lee looked towards Stein, who nodded with approval. He clasped Garf's hand with a nervous shake in his wrist, "It is nice to meet you Garf. My name is Lee Cheng. I was a cleric here in Tristian with my father. He was a monster, so Stein saved me, and now I'm here to help."

An awkward silence fell over the group as eyes fell on Stein.

"Help?" Marlow looked towards Stein, his head tilted in disbelief. "He cured Grekk?"

Stein shook his head, "We don't know if he can be cured."

"Then, we do not need him. He is a child and will either get in the way or be killed. Put him back where you found him." Marlow stomped back towards the corner of the barn, taking a seat atop a barrel.

Lee's eyes fell to the floor. He felt his heart begin to ache at the thought of going back to the grizzly clinic, alone - if it even survived the fire nearby. His mind began to race. *Would people trust coming to a child for treatment, how would he be able to keep the clinic open, how could he buy food?* He would starve. His heart began to pound in his chest.

Garf immediately recognized his sorrow and gently nudged him, "Oh no, don't you let the grumpy-one bring you down to his level. He is too cranky to introduce himself, but that's Marlow - the world's most miserable barn animal."

"Shut up, Garf!" Marlow growled.

"I'm just saying," Garf replied in his slurred speech. He turned back towards Lee, "I don't know your story, Scrap, but no one in here's had it easy. I'm sure you'll do great."

The door to the barn creaked open again, "Did someone say *great*?" Tholden stepped in, throwing his pack to the floor as if to pat his own back. He tossed his head back so that his short hair would bounce atop his head and he equipped a comb from his robe. "I hope you didn't miss me too much."

He was met only by a long sigh.

Tholden scanned the room and then focused on Lee, "Ah, the young cleric. I see you have met my merry band of misfits. What do you think?"

"They are very nice, I like them," Lee smiled.

The last figure from the shrouded corner remained in the shadow. His voice was powerful and carried authority, "You're not our leader, Tholden."

"Well, *I* do seem to be the face of this outfit and *I* do all of the important dealings with the locals. Who better to lead than someone who can handle diplomatic matters?" Tholden argued. "I am the most obvious leader here, being the most cultured and appealing."

"Yes," Grekk said weakly," but no one likes you."

There were snickers from around the barn.

"I could lead once I'm back on my feet," Grekk added.

"Not you, Grekk," Garf said.

There was a communal nod.

Lee felt the nerves finally stop shaking his hands and knees. This group didn't seem to be a group of child-eaters at all, in fact—they seemed rather fun to be around.

"Okay fine," Lee yelled, "I'll do it!"

Stein let out a laugh and it seemed like the entire group had seen his smile for the first time. He reached out to rustle Lee's hair.

The shadowed figure stepped forward into the light, illuminating his crimson scales. His jaw was wide and snout resembled that of a dragon. He had a very broad figure that was outlined by heavy scale armor with accenting furs. The intensity of his yellow eyes brought a chill through Lee's entire body. He spoke with an articulate, deep voice that negated the intimidation of his appearance, "I would follow this little one into battle before I would follow you, Tholden. I can see he has courage—maybe that will rub off on you."

Tholden looked around the group for support and reassurance, but found none. Defeated, he stepped back and sat on a hay bale. He took a moment to brush back his hair, "Very well, Drogon. In that case, we will continue to make group decisions, and hopefully never have a difference of opinion. In the meantime, we must formulate *some* kind of plan, here."

This corner of the barn had primitive seating of arranged hay bales and barrels that centered on a broken shipping crate. Lee could make out mounds of hay that was used for bedding and a decomposing pile of food scraps from previous day's meals. It seemed no one cared much to clean, as the pile had a matching stench that surely everyone could notice.

Marlow, Garf, Tholden and Lee gathered around the center crate while Stein remained standing, leaning against a post. Drogon kept within earshot and began patrolling the barn, peering out through gaps in the boards.

Tholden started, "So we know we are up against a vetala and its corrupted. The master cleric believed this vetala may in fact be a lord or alpha. I will research some lore on more effective hunting strategies, but we should plan to lure it out."

"Oye, I have something." Garf said. "I was able to get a local woman to tell me that the attacks mostly happen in the north. That's in the area of mansions and rich people and whatnot."

Marlow dismissed him, "That woman was a prostitute."

"So?" He argued, "What does that have to do with what she knows? And, she prefers to be called Luscious."

"It's called the Northern Villas, but yes we have now confirmed it with the cleric as well." Tholden nodded and continued, "Clearly, that must be where the lair is. This would then mean that our vetala is one of the nobles of Tristian."

Stein interrupted, "We don't know that. It could just as easily be someone from the commons who resents the lords enough to hunt them. A vetala could still reason and certainly still hate."

"I'll go ask my source," Garf went to stand, but Stein already had a hand pressed down on his shoulder. "Tomorrow then?"

"No." Stein turned and looked towards Lee. "Can you please look in on Grekk? We will need him able to hold a sword as soon as possible."

Lee nodded and went to tend to him at once.

Tholden stood and began to pace. "What if we were to give the vetala the perfect opportunity to slay some noblemen? What if we were to give them a feast to lure them out? Then, we wouldn't have to hunt at all, they would come to us."

"Yes! They would come to thank us," Garf laughed to himself and looked around to a group of stale faces. "No? Is this serious time?"

Tholden continued, "What if we organize some kind of ball, or feast, for all the Lords. We would be there to oversee the entire thing, even watch from rooftops on guests arriving and departing. Surely it would be too easy for the vetala to come out for a snack and we would be ready."

Drogon stopped patrolling and joined the party around the crate. "That's actually *not* a terrible idea. One of us can disguise as a new member of the elite in the neighborhood. This could be the welcoming ball that we are hosting. The rest of us could be in place as guards. Even if things don't go the way we want, we may be able to follow one of them back to their lair – this could work."

"I won't be giving up my axe to dress up and play nobleman," Marlow said quickly.

Garf laughed, "You're too ugly. No one would believe you were noble."

A vicious snarl from Marlow ended the conversation.

"I would say that I am the most obvious choice, being as I am the most cultured." Tholden boasted. "However, in the event I was seen by the fire in town, it may not be wise for me to be the center of attention. Marlow is, well, too conspicuous. Whoever is playing the role will be at the center of the party and likely furthest from the fight when it starts. Stein, you and Drogon are too heavy hitters to not be in the first strike at the vetala."

Meanwhile, Lee had administered all of the available shadowbane to Grekk and began crafting new vials. From across the barn, the opportunity of playing a nobleman hit his ear and he quickly announced, "I can help, I can be a noble!"

"No, you can't." Tholden shook his head. "I wish that it were so simple, but you are too young, you don't know enough."

Lee's excitement faded.

"When you were Lee's age the only spells you knew were to style your hair; but he can reattach severed limbs - want to see?" Stein offered with a smirk. "Lee, you can be the nobleman's son, and that really leaves only Garf to be the noble. Lee will be his son, who will also make sure he remains safe at the party. Tholden, you can stay inside and out of the spotlight to help Garf not to act like a fool. Marlow,

Drogon, and I will be on lookout as Garf's personal guard. Grekk will be a guest at the party to give us more eyes inside in case the vetala is a lord of Tristian. Hopefully, it will also keep him from having to be in the fight. Sound good?"

The entire party turned towards Grekk, who was looking remarkably more rejuvenated. He was slowly getting up to his feet. "I'll be ready," his voice cracked.

Drogon smiled, "Glad to see you're feeling better."

"Yes, great for you," Tholden disregarded him. "It is nearly sunup and we have a lot to do if we are going to have this party tonight: clothing, a mansion that is ours, food and wine. We'll have to split up in order to get this accomplished"

"Whoa, tonight?" Garf argued. "I think we can give it a few days, can't we? How would we even do all that so fast?"

"Every day we wait, more people die and become his corrupted. Besides, I see no reason to delay since we can plan it in a day. A party for nobility is very simple to plan," Tholden mused nonchalantly, "it's just expensive. Invitations could be tricky, but with the right coin we can have some charming locals go door to door and spread the word."

"Oye, fine, but even with all that I'm still a half-breed. Those rich bastards won't see past that for a second," said Garf.

"It's not about that, here, Garf." Tholden explained. "They *will* see right past that when they believe you are the wealthiest man in the city. Trust me. They all will *want* to be your friend."

"Let's go," Drogon said, "Garf, Grekk, and Lee, stay here."

"Wait a minute - I want to come," Lee argued.

Stein walked towards the door and looked back with a smile. "You need to look after Grekk and get some rest. We are going to have a long day tomorrow."

Disappointed, Lee nodded and watched as the barn doors closed in front of him. He heard their voices trailing off as they walked back towards Tristian, delegating duties. He turned to Garf and Grekk, "What do you want to do?"

Grekk rolled over onto a pile of hay with a series of painful groans, a quiet snore rumbled from beneath his cloak.

"Well, Scrap, Stein is right. You've probably been through a lot today and it's only just begun. Maybe some sleep would do you some good, you think?"

"But I want to help," Lee protested.

Garf sat him down and began to pile up some hay into child-size bedding. "You won't be much help if you're not rested up. Tell you what; just lay down for an hour, and I'll tell Stein you slept all night, deal?"

"Okay," Lee sat down on his straw bed and leaned back, his hands behind his head. He was quiet for a few minutes before his mind began to race with images of blood, flesh, and fire. He didn't even realize he said it until it was too late. "Garf, can you tell me a story."

"A story?" Garf said with a laugh. "I don't know if I know any stories, I'm not that good at them. How old are you anyway?"

"I'm twelve, but that doesn't mean I don't like stories. It'll help me not think about my own." He looked up from his straw pallet, "I just don't think I can take my mind off everything and go to sleep. Please? It's been a rough day."

"I've been there before," Garf replied. He looked down at Lee for a moment and noticed the shine of tears pooling in young Lee's eyes. "Oh boy, what kind of story do you want?"

"Well," he pondered, "I want to know about Stein. He said he would take care of me since my father was a monster. And, he told me some things about himself. But I don't think he told me everything."

"What are you talking about, exactly?" Garf asked.

"I asked Stein why he had stitches all over him and he said it was because he fights a lot. I asked him why he has tattoos and he said he was born with them. I asked him where he got his scythe and he said he won it in a duel," Lee said, "it just seems like there's more to those stories."

"He said he won it in a duel?" Garf laughed and was quickly still. "Actually, I guess you could say he won it."

Lee shot up, "I want to know! Please tell me."

"All right, don't get so excited. I'm not sure Stein would be okay with me telling you, so you didn't hear it from me, got it?" Garf waited for an agreement before continuing.

Lee nodded.

"Everything he told you is true, but you're right, Scrap, it's not the *whole* story. He was born with those tattoos. All kai people are born with tattoos that show their destiny. I know that only the kai who bears them can read them – and only at a certain point in their life. Other than that, I don't know much about it." Garf rubbed the side of his head as if still searching for information. "Stein does fight. He fights a lot, but those scars aren't from battles. Not all of them, anyway. He was used for experiments, by his own father no less."

"Why would he do that?" asked Lee.

"I know that his father is King Treyalt and he–"

Lee interrupted, "The King of the Radiant Empire? That would make Stein a prince!"

Garf continued, "He is a prince. It's not like anyone would recognize him with all those scars and in those torn up robes. Not to mention he sleeps in a barn with roughnecks like us."

Lee was confused. "Why did he do that to Stein—to his own son?"

He hesitated to answer, "You better not rat me out for telling you this stuff."

"I promise, I won't say anything," Lee assured him.

Garf stared into his eyes. "All right, you better not. I would be in trouble with him if he found out." He sighed, "Oh boy, where was I?"

"Stein as a prince, duh."

"Alright, simmer down," he joked, "Yeah, that's right. See, King Treyalt was sick with some rare illness. The best clerics in the kingdom couldn't fix him and they were running out of time. The clerics said that they needed to do tests to find a cure, but the tests were very risky and could kill him. Since Stein was of the same blood and the last in line for the throne, King Treyalt and the clerics infected Stein to use him for these tests instead. It was inhuman what they did to him. They cut him up, tore him apart, and stitched him back together until they found something that would save the king."

Lee's eyes were wide, "How did he do it? How did live through all that?"

"The clerics kept healing him to keep him alive for more tests; it was the worst kind of torture. You see, just because they couldn't cure the disease each time didn't mean they couldn't patch him up or take care of all the bleeding and try again- but you are right though, Scrap; that this was a torture that tears your mind apart and drives you mad. To answer your question– he didn't make it. Stein *died* after all those tests."

Lee lowered his brow. "You're being stupid, Stein isn't dead."

Garf said, "No, not anymore."

"Someone resurrected him, then? One of the clerics?" Lee said.

"He resurrected himself," Garf answered. "Sort of."

Lee leaned back and rolled his eyes. "This is ridiculous, are you making this up?"

"No way am I making it up. Do you *really* think I could make up this stuff? Listen, Stein died after all those tests and when he died a reaper came to, I don't know, reap him?" His shrug showed that he didn't really understand. "You know, take him to the underworld, or into the next life—or whatever it is that happens."

"Go on, what happened?" Pressed Lee.

"Well, Stein was furious with his father and the clerics. He wasn't ready to pass on, but the reaper—well his job is to take the dead. So, Stein told the reaper, 'no' and the reaper said, 'yes'. And they fought it out, right there in spirit realm."

Lee was now sitting up in bed with his mouth hanging open.

Garf continued, "Stein was a vengeful spirit, made up of pure hatred. He is a tough nut in the living world, so I'd imagine his angry ghost would be just as strong. I don't know how it works or how it's even possible, but somehow he was able to kill the reaper. When he did, he took the reaper's scythe and cloak and was able to step back into the world of the living."

Lee shouted, "That's amazing!"

"You're telling me," he said, "I don't know how you could take down a reaper, but if anyone could, it would be Stein– or Drogon, I guess."

"Can you tell me a story about Drogon?" Lee asked.

Garf pushed Lee's head down softly, "Another night, Scrap. Besides, I don't want to get in trouble with him, too. Get some sleep. And, remember, you didn't hear *any* of this from me."

Lee laid down and turned onto his side. Before closing his eyes he whispered, "I won't say anything. Good night, Garf."

His mind raced, no longer with the real-life horrors of today, but with the thought of an epic battle between Stein and a reaper. He could dream the sway of the reapers cloak; completely enshrouding his figure and face, and the scorching flame emanating off its scythe. Stein, furious and defiant, staring him down in princely rags.

"I have come to claim you," said the reaper in a trailing whisper, "your life has ended, and it is time for me to ferry you into your afterlife."

"No," Stein said, sheer rage burning in his eyes, "I will not be thrown into a hole with the worms before I devour the very heart of those who damned me here!"

Lee lay twitching on his straw pallet, the dream filling his sleep with Stein and the Reaper.

The reaper hovered closer through the air, embers dropping off the blade and scorching the grayed earth beneath them, "Many feel as you feel, Stein. That they have been taken before their time. Victims of life and her great circumstance. You are not alone in thinking this. However, I can assure you. However unnatural your death, this is your time. It has been foretold by the prophecy of the **Maker** and that is how I am here to greet you."

"No," said Stein.

"I understand how you feel," the reaper whispered.

"No," said Stein.

"Others have felt the same way," the reaper continued.

"No!" Stein's voice thundered, echoing through this hollow place. He charged forward with a leap and soared through the air as if weightless. His single bound brought him above the reaper. He led with his fist and swung into its head with a downward thrust. The reaper plummeted, crashing into the ground below forcefully, but landing on its feet.

It slid, and braced to a stop as its hood flew from its head. Staring back from the cracked eye socket of a skull was a red glowing eye. Sliding back its left foot and taking a stance, it beckoned him, "Your soul is mine, to claim or destroy, what do you prefer?"

Stein's face twitched. His eyes glared, his teeth snarled, with his mind fixated, not on life or death, but the most gruesome revenge. There were no other thoughts, no doubts, or fears, or the possibility of non-existence as he charged at the reaper again.

IV

Planning a Party

"A wise strategy is worth more than a thousand warriors."
The Wayward Warrior – A Tribute to Solihart.

The sun rose over the hills of Tristian. Beams of light illuminated thin dashes through missing planks in the barn roof. Lee sat up, rubbing his eyes and looked around. Grekk was still snoring away where he passed out the night before, but no one else was here. Lee could see movement outside through the spacing of the boards and heard a faint exchange of familiar voices. He slid his boots on and got up to join them.

Lee slid open the barn door and was greeted by Stein and Tholden petting two large stallions. The first stallion was snowy white and wore a small nameplate, *Dash*. The second stallion was finely brushed and black haired. On his chest plate displayed the name *Constantine*. Both stood together, attached to an ornate black carriage with golden trim. The sun reflected brilliantly off the shine of the paint, forcing Lee to squint, before he looked away.

"Good morning, young cleric," greeted Tholden. "Did you sleep all right?"

Lee stopped and stared at the stallions before approaching Constantine. "They are beautiful. He looks so strong. And I have never seen a carriage as fancy as this one." He held up his hand to Constantine, who lowered his head and met Lee's palm with a dry lick. "Gross!" Lee giggled, without moving his hand away.

"Yes, yes, well tonight is the grand ball to introduce Lord Garfus of Gashimar as a new resident here in Tristian. The more coin he has, the more nobles will come to try and befriend him. Fickle creatures, the nobles." Tholden laughed. "We purchased an estate in the Northern Villas and Marlow is there now with some hired help, making sure the place is all cleaned up. It's going to be—quite—a night."

Lee was now grinning and giggling with one hand being licked by Constantine, and one by Dash. "This is going to be so fun, I can't wait! What can I do? I want to help."

Stein smiled, as if he was waiting for him to ask. "For you, we have a very special job. Remember yesterday, when I asked you if you want to be the son of a nobleman? Well, I meant it. Lord Garfus –" he smirked at the thought, "is up at the main house with the tailor. He is waiting for you to get fitted for the big night."

Lee jumped up. "Thank you! I won't let you down."

"Go on, they're waiting for you," Stein encouraged.

Lee turned and scampered to run up the hill towards the main house. He was wiping his hands on his robes the whole way up to the house.

Tholden waited until Lee was out of earshot. "Clever idea, Stein. He gets to feel special that he is playing a nobleman's child, Garf is there to look after him, and he is furthest from the fight when something happens. From time to time you remind me you're not all brawn without brain."

"You know me," said Stein.

"Tell me something, what is your plan with him?" Tholden asked.

"Plan? What makes you think I have a plan for him?" he said.

"You told me before you were just doing 'the right thing,' but I know there has got to be more to it than that. I have seen you take a bite from a man's heart—literally—mind you. You can't expect me to believe you have soft spot for this kid, do you?"

Stein turned and began walking towards the main house.

"Seriously?" Tholden shouted. "Fine, we'll talk later."

At the main house, Lee burst through the door to see Garf standing with his arms straight out. He was wearing a black suit, made up of glistening silk with gold trim, as well as an *almost* an excessive amount of rhinestones. A slender elf was measuring and pulling at the sleeves, which only added Garf's frustrated look to the ensemble.

His eye caught Lee in the mirror and his cheeks bloomed red. "Oh great, came to watch me dress a fool in these rich pants, did you? Well go on—get your laughs out now, Scrap."

Lee stared at him, eyes scanning up and down. He did not know Garf long, but gathered he never cleaned himself up, no less dressed in anything better than *lightly* soiled clothing. Yet, here he stood—a tailored three-piece suit, with rhinestone and gold trim, a gold pocket watch, and his scalp shaved and shined. "Garf—Lord Garfus, I think you look very noble. I hope I can pull it off like you do."

Garf said, "Nah, you're just saying that. No man looks good in pretty-lady clothes. My head looks like a polished butt."

"No, really!" Lee said, "If I am going to be your son, I want a suit to match. And maybe we can make the Garfus family insignia on the back with gold trim or jewels?"

The elf began tapping her foot rapidly. "We have no time for that kind of alteration if you need this for tonight. It will be a struggle to sew it together to fit you properly. With only half a days' notice, customizations are out of the question."

"Oh, that would've been really nice," Lee sighed.

"That's okay, Scrap. I have another family trinket I could give you." Garf reached back and pulled out a dagger from tucked into his belt. It was in a hard, lightwood sheath that was bare, except for a few splits in the sides. "I got this from my dad a long time ago. It was my first dagger. Why don't you keep it—like a family heirloom, or whatever?"

Lee pulled the sheath open to expose the tattered, but sharpened blade. "Really? Are you sure you won't miss it?"

"Oye, my dad was a bastard. It'd be good to be rid of it. Slip it up your sleeve and it packs quite a nasty backswing; so be careful. This little knife saved my skin more than a dozen times. Take care of it, eh?" Garf winked. "Oh, and you didn't get it from me."

Lee nodded gratefully and tucked it in his robes.

"I'm done with you, Lord Garfus," said the elf. "Your turn, young master, Lee. What are you looking to wear this evening?"

He pointed at Garf, "That. But my size, please."

"I see." The elf approached Garf with a whisper, "My lord, these silks and trim are imported from Gashimar. I do have enough to make the boy a matching suit but the coin –"

"The boy wants *this* suit and I have the coin. So, dress the boy." Garf gave Lee a wink and sat down.

"Yes, my lord," she said. She gathered the lengths of silk and draped them over Lee's slender form. The jacket fell loosely, and the too-long pants puddled at his feet. The elf then began to pin them for sizing, tossing the pieces away that were no longer needed. It was coming together as a smaller version of Garf's elegant clothing.

A few minutes into the sizing the door creaked opened, allowing the morning sun to beam into the mirror. Lee closed his eyes and when the door shut, he opened his eyes to see Stein in the reflection.

"Stein, look at my clothes!" He waved his hands with the too-long sleeves swinging wildly. He stopped, stood with his chin in the air, and spoke in a sophisticated tone, "I am a noble, and this noble would like some pancakes."

Stein smiled, "Are you hungry? I'm sure Tholden could make something up for us."

He relaxed from his noble demeanor, "Yeah, of course, but does he know how to make pancakes?"

"I'm sure he does. He uses magic for everything, including making breakfast. Garf, does Tholden know how to make pancakes?"

Garf was staring at Stein with his mouth hanging open, "In all our time together, I hadn't seen you smile until yesterday. Then again, just now—you al'right?"

Stein's face became stern. "Come back to the barn when you're done here. I'll tell Tholden to get ready for breakfast." He turned and made his way outside.

"Can we go eat, please?" Lee asked the tailor.

"I suppose you could. I have pinned you up well enough, go on," she replied.

"Garf, let's go please, please," he said, "Pancakes!"

Without hesitation, Garf stood and threw his silks to the tailor. "You don't gotta tell me twice."

Back near the barn, Lee and Garf approached the group outside at an improvised table. It was crudely assembled from spare planks and barrels. Already sitting was Tholden, Stein, Drogon and Grekk. From a distance, the men appeared engaged in deep conversation, leaning over their makeshift table. As Garf and Lee approached, those at the table stopped their discussion, looked over and, at once, relaxed into more casual positions when they saw who it was.

"Lord Garfus and the young master," Tholden joked, "have you come for your noble breakfast?"

"Yes please," Lee replied. "Tholden, Stein said you might know how to make pancakes?"

Tholden looked towards Stein with an eyebrow raised, "Well, you are informed correctly, young master. Is that what your heart desires?"

"By the maker, yes!" Lee yelled.

Tholden began to swirl his hands in the air and orbs of orange energy grew in the space around them. Like the crashing of flint rock, sparks ignited the orbs and created plates that set themselves around the table at each seating. After the plates came napkins, then forks, and drinking glasses. The orbs continued to swirl as Tholden kept his hands in motion, and with each spark came a soft pop as a container of syrup appeared, followed by pancakes with strips of ham appeared on each plate.

No one at the table seemed impressed. It was as if they had seen it a hundred times. All except for Lee, who sat in amazement with his jaw slackened. "How did you – that's impossible. You can't create something from nothing. No one can. That's the first rule of magic."

Tholden grinned from ear to ear, "Except for those of rare and extraordinary abilities, like those of the Moonstorm family. I—would—offer to teach you, but some talents you just have to be born with and can't be taught. Some of us are just born of this level of greatness."

Stein's eyes locked onto Tholden, a look that the rest of the party knew as a threat. Everyone froze in place. He paused for a moment. Then, calmly as coldly, with a solemn ferocity he said, "Speak down to him again, and I will-"

Drogon interrupted, "I believe that Tholden meant he has a few years on you, Lee. With practice and support from us, I'm sure you'll be even *more* talented than Tholden. And, I don't say that just to make you feel better. I say it because we believe in you."

Stein's eyes remained fixed onto Tholden.

"Do you mean that?" Lee looked up to him.

"Of course. Stein has taken you into our family and you are one of us. For better or worse, but let's face it—you make us better. Believe in yourself, Lee. That will be the source of your true power." Drogon held out his claw-like hand and in his palm danced a green, sparkling light. It began to twirl as it took to the shape of a small glowing tigertail. It spun slowly in his hand for a moment before he allowed it to dissipate, causing a small shower of green dust. "Control and discipline— you can manipulate any spell if you have those."

Lee recognized the spell as being one of minor healing but had never thought to try to manipulate it beyond what he was taught. He listened intently, impressed that this brute of a **dragonkin** could wield magic at all. "Thank you, Drogon," he said at last, "that means a lot to me."

Drogon nodded and pulled his sword from his sheath. A golden glow from his hand passed into the hilt and ran through the length of the blade. "And when you are ready, even unlock magic that is imbued or hidden."

Lee looked on in amazement, "Your sword is magical? How did you do that?"

"Yes. When it was forged, Rayne was enchanted with holy magic. As a paladin, I can tap into the magic that was enchanted into it." He laughed. "First you learn the art, and then you learn to use it. When you're ready, you as a natural-born cleric could tap into the magic from Rayne or anything like her."

"Her?" Lee asked. "Rayne is a *her*?"

"The one who enchanted it was a woman; therefore, the energy and the magic inside it is that of a woman." Drogon answered. "We can study together another time, if you want to."

"Of course!" Lee smiled.

Stein had yet to lower his piercing glare off of Tholden, who was making every effort to dodge his eyes by feathering and brushing his hair. This continued for the remainder of breakfast. When everyone had finished, Tholden waved his hands again and bits of orange light danced around to clean and disintegrate plates, as well as any scraps of food.

"Thank you, Tholden," Drogon said warmly.

"Thank you!" praised Lee.

Tholden gave a wave of his hand and a subtle nod. He seemed more reserved, for the time being.

"Everything is fitting into place and tonight we will have the grand ball in your name, Lord Garfus." Drogon bowed towards Garf. He reached into his pack and began handing out pamphlets that advertised *Lord Garfus's Grand Homecoming Event*. "Marlow is finishing the final preparations at the estate, so all we will need to do is rest up, get ourselves ready and head there tonight. Do you all know where you need to be?"

"This is what was given out to the nobles?" said Tholden.

"Yes, this was the invitation. Believe me, when they saw all the servants and decorations we were bringing in – everyone will be there," Drogon said.

"Everyone?" Lee asked.

"Every noble lord in the Northern Villas will be there. It was very important that we keep the guests exclusively upper class and it will certainly lure out the creature," Drogon replied.

Grekk looked curiously at the invitation, "What is the **Path of Rubies**? Is that a bank or something?"

"I didn't even notice that - the Path of Rubies is the street for the wealthiest of Tristian!" Lee said with excitement. "How did you manage to buy an estate in a day, on the fanciest street in town?"

"It wasn't cheap," said Drogon. "Lord Garfus and young master Lee will be the center of attention. Your main role will be to convince everyone you are of nobility, so do your best to act the part. If you notice anything out of the ordinary, tell one of us. Remember, we are your muscle and will take care of anything. Our goal is to keep you as non-combatants unless things get out of control. Grekk, this includes y-"

Lee interrupted, "Wait, I'm not allowed to help?"

"You are helping by acting as the son of a nobleman," said Stein.

"But I want to *actually* help," Lee argued.

Drogon looked at him and spoke softly, "I need you to help Garf pull this off, and he can't do it alone. You are smart and capable, as well as clever. I know you can do it, but I need to know you are committed. Can I trust you to see this through?"

Lee hesitated. He had never really been spoken to like an adult—an adult who was part of a team. "Yes, you can." He felt Stein's supportive hand grip his shoulder.

"Thank you, Lee." Drogon nodded with reassurance. "Grekk, you are a guest from **Gashimar**. I would like for you to mingle with the locals and see if you can help us narrow down a few key targets."

"I can do that," he said.

"Tholden, you are Lord Garfus's advisor. Please make sure Garf does as little public speaking as possible." Drogon pleaded.

"I figured I would say Lord Garfus has a heavy accent since he was raised Gashimar. This would explain why he sounds so uneducated and why he needs me to interpret what the nobles would feel is common culture," Tholden explained.

Garf didn't seem to notice he was being insulted

Drogon looked on at Garf, who was watching the grass sway in a gust of wind. "That is actually a perfect idea. Marlow and I will be your doormen, checking invitations and keeping an eye out street level. If there is any action, we will be first in the fight. If nothing happens on its own, we will meet up with Garf in a few hours in to discuss any leads."

Stein rose up a scarred hand, "Am I not invited?"

Drogon snickered, "Of course you're invited, but I don't see the need to tell you where to be since I know you won't follow through with *any* plan."

The entire table let out a laugh in agreement.

Drogon continued with a serious tone, "Move around as you wish, Stein, you will be dressed as a guard. I ask only that you don't engage the creature alone."

He nodded.

"Then we are all set for tonight," said Drogon. "Sharpen your blades, pray for strength, and get some rest. It's going to be a long night."

They stood from the table and quietly moved into the barn to find their respective hay piles. Lee rested his head on an old blanket he was using as an improvised pillow, smiling at the thought of how this band of intimidating warriors was taking time to nap before battle. He wasn't even sure if he could fall asleep until he felt his breathing slow and his eyelids grow heavier and heavier.

Lee seemed to only close his eyes a few minutes ago when he was awakened by the others stirring. Hours had passed and the nap was over. He sat up to see through a missing plank that the sun had painted the sky a hue of purples and orange that dimly lit the inside of the barn. The party was getting dressed in their new formal clothing. Lee got to his feet and brushed the straw from his hair. His three-piece suit neatly hung from a rusty nail.

He glanced around the room to observe how everyone else cleaned up and was impressed by what he saw. Marlow and Drogon were in shined black leather armor that had a matching gold trimming to Garf's robe pattern. They appeared as finely tailored yet formidable mercenaries. Garf had somehow managed to keep his ensemble clean and pressed, although he seemed to pay little regard to keeping it that way from the reckless manner in which he was stowing knives within every fold. Grekk was wearing a dark brown tunic with an orange undershirt. He appeared to have regained most of the color in his scales and was very energetic. Tholden's robe was purple with yellow and orange accents. On his lapel was a purple crescent moon with a remarkably detailed face pressed into it. While Lee admired it from a distance, the face on Tholden's clothing winked at him and then froze back into place.

Lee was startled, first by the face, and then by the hand on his shoulder. He turned to see Stein. "Hi Stein, are you excited for the party?"

Stein was dressed in a pressed robe styled to match Drogon and Marlow's guard outfits. Looking closer, Lee could see this was Stein's same **deathrobe** that was cleaned and decorated with a similar trim. Stein knelt down and straightened Lee's collar, "Tonight, I want you to stay with Garf and have a good time at the party. Should anything happen, you stay with one of us and I will find you after, okay?"

"Okay, Stein, but I can help. If I am there with you, I can heal you if you get hurt. If I wasn't there and something happened, I wouldn't be able to forgive myself. This is my family now and I need to help."

Stein nodded with approval, "I know what you mean, but if you were there with me, in the middle of it all, and something happened to you, I couldn't forgive myself either. The safest place for you is inside with Garf."

Lee felt discouraged, "Okay, but then you have to promise me you will be careful. You have to promise me you'll come back. Can you promise?"

He hesitated, "I promise."

Tholden had slid open the barn door and stepped into the opening. He looked out into the sunset. "This is it gentlemen, the hour is upon us—last chance to leave town." He let out a bold laugh. "Don't worry though, I will see us through. We may pick on each other, but know that I will be looking out for each and every one of you."

There was a silence until Drogon finally spoke, "Well, I feel better already."

Laughter erupted from the barn.

"Excuse me for trying to be an inspirational!" Tholden said while stepping out of the barn.

The party followed out behind him to the stagecoach. It looked even more elaborate in the dim light and seemed to reflect every color in the sky. Dash and Constantine stood proudly, appearing as if they, too, spent the afternoon preparing for whatever was about to happen. Drogon and Marlow sat up top while the rest climbed inside. As soon as the door had shut, there was a soft tap of the reins as the carriage moved forward.

No one spoke for most of the ride. The tension was rife as everyone rehearsed in their minds what they had to do. Tholden was still upset from being laughed at, and Stein seemed angry being so close to him. Garf was tense, trying not to move in an effort to preserve his clothing and it made him look stiff. Grekk was staring out the side window, as if deep in thought.

Lee turned to Grekk, "You are looking much better, how do you feel?"

Though Lee hadn't known many reptilians, he could see the grin of a smile on Grekk's elongated snout. "Much better thanks to you. I owe you my life, Lee."

Lee smiled and rubbed his head. "It was nothing, and you're welcome. You are looking better, but you've been quiet. Is everything all right?"

Grekk let out a sigh, "I was thinking about a girl I used to date."

"You dated someone?" Tholden scoffed.

"She was Ayla's daughter, Leliana. That's actually how I knew we could use her barn when we got here. She could use the extra coin and she is someone we can trust. It was a long time ago," his voice trailed off.

"Yes," Tholden rubbed his chin. "I did think it was unusual that you wanted to handle our sleeping arrangement, for once. The fact that you were able to guarantee her discretion was also impressive, but now I see why."

"That's why I did it, I knew Ayla from when I dated Leliana. I wanted to do the talking alone because we have this bit of history. I didn't want to cause her any grief," Grekk said, "I would've taken us elsewhere if she wasn't comfortable with it."

Tholden was intrigued, "Why was it uneasy? Did you guys have a bad breakup? She decided she didn't like your claws on her anymore?"

"No," Grekk said softly, "she died."

Tholden was silent.

Lee put a hand on his arm. "I'm really sorry, Grekk. I'm sure she was happy just to have met you and share the time with you."

"No, that's probably not true either," he paused, "I'm the reason she's dead."

Lee wasn't sure what to say but kept his hand on him.

"I don't want to talk about it. I just think about her sometimes and being back in that barn makes it all come flashing back," Grekk said.

"If you ever change your mind, I'm a good listener," Lee said.

Grekk smiled, "I appreciate that, Lee, but I think it's best she remains in my memories."

The coach came to a stop. There was a loud cheering outside accompanied by a thunderous applause. Stein reached to grab the door handle and turned to the group, "Is everyone ready? Lord Garfus?"

Lee could read their faces—they were excited. Somewhere among this crowd could be a demon, an evil vetala accompanied by its enslaved corrupted. All of them knew that this night would only be successful if it ended in bloodshed. They could only be finished with this quest and the village would only be safe if the monster was slain. Something about this thought made Lee uneasy. He wondered if a curse could be broken, and if the monster could be saved, rather than destroyed. He wanted to speak of mercy but recognized that he was among these great hunters and held his tongue.

Garf took a slow deep breath, "Aye."

Everyone gave a confirming nod as they stepped out to meet their guests and perhaps among them; death itself.

A Feast of Nobles

"Only the victor may tell the tales of battle."
The Flail of Korthus – A Tribute to Korthus.

As the door to the carriage swung open, the cheering from the crowd grew louder with anticipation. There were more than one hundred people dressed in fine clothing, wearing the most elaborate jewelry and flattering smiles. They were eager to grab the attention of this wealthy new lord from Gashimar and crowded the Path of Rubies outside to surround them.

Marlow and Drogon leaped down from the coach and began parting the sea of people with gentle shoving. "Stand back and make way," they said.

Stein climbed out to help and began to open a path with only the threatening chill of his stare.

Next out was Tholden, who stood on the carriage step and gestured his hands with palms down to silence the guests. He announced, "Ladies and gentlemen, thank you all for coming and especially on such short notice. I shouldn't be surprised—I always heard the lords and ladies of Tristian were ones who always knew how to party." His words were met with laughter and cheering. "Yes, and I won't be the one to keep you from your wine and merriment. Without further ado, it is with my utmost honor and pleasure to introduce Lord Garfus of Gashimar and his son—the young master, Lee."

A roar of excitement erupted as Garf and Lee stepped out of the carriage. Their matching outfits made this young human and half-breed look a part of nobility and kinship better than the group could have hoped for. The guests were wholly convinced and shouted approval.

Drogon and Marlow took their position outside the front door and began to form the guests into lines to check their invitations. Garf and Lee walked through the narrowing pathway and made it into the estate vestibule alone. Both stared with wide eyes at the beauty and décor of the building. First, they were greeted by the seductive blend of spices that accompanied the slow cooked meats from the next room. It was also decorated in the epitome of elegance. The entrance hall had a raised thirty-foot ceiling with crystal chandeliers hanging above. Every wall had a large portrait of Garf standing in powerful poses. One of the portraits showed him wrestling a bull to the ground by its horns. While in another, he was lifting an elderly gnome.

Their steps echoed on the marble floor as Garf and Lee slowly strolled through the foyer and into the main hall. Servants bowed as they passed.

Lee noticed Stein had followed them in and felt comfortable enough to ask about something that was on his mind. While they still had privacy, he spoke, "I know people will be coming in any second, but I have to know—how did you guys afford all of this?"

Garf was still staring up at the ceilings admiring a sophistication that he couldn't understand. "I hate to tell you, Scrap, but I have no idea. I don't deal with the coin, that's more of Tholden's thing. I'm sure it has something to do with counterfeiting coin. That normally works for us."

"Can't people tell?" Lee asked.

Garf shrugged, "Tholden is good at what he does when he wants to be. He picks up some rocks and uses a spell to make them look like gold coins. A clever or magical person can see through it, but someone like me might not notice until the magic has worn off, sometimes a week later. Don't worry, we'll be gone by then."

They entered the main hall. It was as massive as a warehouse and was capped with a great dome. The dome was an obsidian glass, decorated with an image of the night sky - but even this was illuminated by magic. Stars flickered about the glass and a green-eyed moon danced the sky. Lee recognized the image from the stories of **Luna, the Moon Goddess**. Around her, a fiery shooting star and two smaller stars orbited through space in an infinite heart shaped pattern. Lee smiled as he thought of her story. Then, the image of a **star**

serpent caught his attention as it wove around other planets. On the far side of the hall was a long buffet table offering a display cheeses, fruits, vegetables and dips. Huge bouquets of flowers of orange and purple assortment adorned the center of each table. Stacked beside it was a tower of champagne glasses that beckoned as the entering guests to surround the bar. A band of musicians dressed in purple and gold velvet started playing melodies meant to seduce and relax the guests. The servants began offering sweetmeats and cocktails to the gorgeous dressed attendees.

An hour passed.

Garf was able to keep up the confident act of a nobleman, and for the time being, it appeared as if the lords were satisfied with Tholden as his interpreter. Most of Garf's conversation centered on his great entrepreneurial success. Many were begging to see if he would be willing to do business with them. Tholden improvised a **gaweed** plantation back in Gashimar that led the noblemen to believe that Garf held the wealth of a small nation. By the time Tholden was done spinning his tales, *Garfus Gaweed* was the source of all gaweed in the world—leaving him with power to topple nations overnight.

Stein and Grekk were walking the room, quietly observing anyone that could be the vetala lord in disguise. Their approach was quite different from one another. Grekk was carrying on conversations with the guests and working the room. Stein would greet most questions with a cold stare that seemed to make people uncomfortable.

The tower of champagne had dismantled to become an assortment of glasses - a testament to the passing of the hours. Drogon and Marlow entered the main hall and found their way over to Garf. They signaled to the group to gather around.

They placed themselves in the corner of the room, making sure to be out of earshot of any guests. Drogon spoke first, "I have two men in mind, Lord Vulcan the kai, and Master Kodor the dragonkin."

"Interestingly enough, Vulcan was my mark so far," Grekk agreed, "his complexion is quite pale for a kai, and there was a way he moved. It seemed almost like every move he made was deliberate. I didn't notice anything about Kodor."

"All kai have that complexion, look at Stein," Tholden said.

"Not all, so that doesn't make him less suspect," said Grekk.

"That was half of your reasoning, Grekk. I'm simply stating it doesn't make him more a suspect, either," Tholden responded.

They studied him from across the room. He was of a lighter kai complexion that looked as a pale gray. Present over his body were natural kai markings that resembled tribal tattoos. They extended up the left side of his face and down his neck. His long, black hair was nearly shoulder length and there was a crescent bald spot at the front of his hairline. He was wearing a royal blue tunic with thick gold bangles up each arm. Staring longer, they could see that he moved with slow and conscious gestures. It was as if he was steadying himself with each movement.

Drogon spoke, "If he is an Alpha, I'm sure he is incredibly fast. Maybe he has to slow himself down for regular interactions like this? Do you have another lead, Tholden?"

"No," he answered sharply, "I was stuck babysitting this imbecile."

"*I'm* part Orc," Garf responded.

This irrelevant response was met with a brief silence.

Tholden looked on with disgust, "see what I mean?"

Drogon continued, "Marlow, anything?"

He scoffed and gave an affirming nod. "I don't know. Figure it out and let me know who gets my axe tonight."

"No surprise there—the bull didn't notice anyone. What exactly were you doing when you met *literally everyone* while taking invitations?" scolded Tholden.

"Never mind," Marlow said, "Tholden is the creature."

"I agree," said Stein with a curt smile.

"Enough, all of you," Drogon said, "did you notice anyone, Lee?"

At this moment, Lee realized that throughout this entire party he had not for a single moment, been looking out for the vetala lord. He had danced with several lords and ladies, briefly picked at a lute that a band member left unattended, and had just enough time to eat half a plate of imported Gashimar cheese pastries. He didn't even consider that he was going to be called on for information. He stood quiet and blushed with embarrassment.

"It's Vulcan," Stein said with confidence.

"How can you be so sure?" Tholden asked.

"I noticed his movements, but I also noticed his dates. He came in with a human and an elf woman who both have the same pale-gray complexion and the same deliberate movements. They are vetaless," Stein explained.

The joyous rhythm of the band no longer fit with the silent dread from the party.

"So, we have one lord, two vetaless, and who knows how many corrupted," Drogon listed. "At least the important ones are here, right now. This is the time to strike."

Marlow began reaching for his axe until Tholden grabbed his arm. "Wait, we don't know if this is all of them. Are you willing to give up our element of surprise with only what we know right now?"

"What are you thinking?" Drogon said.

Tholden looked around suspiciously and whispered, "Why don't we finish out the party and follow them back to their nest. We can size them up from there and attack them at the very hole they crawled out of. They would have no retreat, and no warning."

"Then we run the risk of being outnumbered and losing our chance at the lord. Here we will have the advantage." Drogon urged.

"So—now then?" Marlow continued reaching for his axe.

Tholden grabbed him again, "No, then we put these people at risk by bringing on a battle with an Alpha."

Marlow snarled at him.

Stein turned towards the nobles, "They are already in danger, and they *will* be until Vulcan is dead."

"I agree," said Drogon as he equipped the sword and shield from his back.

Marlow growled in triumph, finally clutching the shaft of his great axe.

Tholden sighed, "They *already* are in danger."

Garf looked to the others and patted himself down. "I-I have no weapon."

"Weren't you stuffing knives into every fold of your robes?" Tholden asked.

"I took them out. You told me to look like a noble, and a noble wouldn't have knives in his robes," said Garf.

There was no reaction; it was as if no one was surprised that Garf was coming to face down a vetala unarmed.

Lee reached out a familiar lightwood dagger, "I think you need this still, huh?"

He grabbed it, "I'm just going to borrow it. You can have it back later."

"That's fine," Lee replied, "I'm just going to hang back."

Stein stepped out into the center of the dance floor, staring down Vulcan from across the massive room. "Party's over!" he shouted.

The band instinctively stopped playing as a hush fell over the guests.

"Now, get out!" Stein slid back his foot and crouched into a stance. He held his empty hands out in front of him, the air igniting in his grip to summon his long-crooked scythe. There was a crackle of magical energy as the blade erupted into an arc of flame across the blade.

The guests near him were pushed back by the powerful burst of heat. At once, many began screaming and sprinting towards the door. They were tripping over each other, knocking over chairs and tables, dashing between other nobles who were frozen in shock.

The group was in line with Stein, weapons drawn and centered onto Vulcan. Lee stood behind them, concentrating small green balls of swirling energy, ready to mend his allies. Tholden's palms were surrounded by spinning fire. To their surprise, of the one hundred guests, only thirty of them ran out screaming from the madman with the flaming scythe. The remaining guests were standing in place, staring at them.

"Get out!" Marlow roared. His voice carried with such intensity—it rattled every empty glass in the hall.

Suddenly, the remaining guests burst out in laughter. They were keeling over, grabbing their sides, and slapping at their knees. The nobles were in outright hysterics at the obvious threat Marlow and Stein just made. Vulcan remained unmoved on the far side of the room, wearing a long smirk across the dark markings on his face.

"No," Vulcan said. As he spoke, the nobles were silenced. They parted in front of him as he slowly walked towards the group. "I think this party has only just begun."

"It can't be. All of them are corrupted? *All* of them?" Tholden mumbled.

"It was too easy," Vulcan continued forward, loosely discarding his robes and formal attire, "this cesspool of a city is mine and I will make it great. I will take every soul. I will bleed out every drop - down to the last rat in the commons." His muscles began to tear and stretch, bulking his body and lengthening his very skeleton. He twisted and jerked, manipulating his body to twice the height and broadness of even Marlow. His eyes glazed over black with a small red pupil that fixed onto the scythe. Then, they met Steins. He stared into him, "What is your name, kai?"

"Stein," he answered.

"Stein, that is an *impressive* weapon you hold there. How did you manage to come across that?" asked Vulcan.

Stein held his ground as the vetala grew closer. "I pried it from the grip of a reaper as I killed him."

"That's impressive," his voice trailed, "I don't suppose you would hand it over? I would hate to see it fade back into the void if I choose to kill you. Unlike others, I would put it to real use."

"You want my scythe?" Stein asked.

"Yes, perhaps we can make a deal. Barter the safety of your companions for the scythe?" Vulcan insisted.

Stein remained motionless, "*This* scythe?"

"Yes, you fool—do you have any other? I want it and I will have it." He snarled as a wet slobber dangled from the corner of his mouth.

Stein erupted, "Then I will give it to you!"

In the same instant, he dashed forward in a blur of motion and soared through the air. He leapt twenty feet high and far enough to clear the dance floor. The wide swing of his crooked blade was brought across Vulcan's face with a deep gash from the top of his cheek to the bottom of his chin. The wound spurted thick black essence that left Vulcan clasping at his face.

"Kill them!" He shouted, "Take everything from them!"

The remaining lords and ladies let out an ear-piercing shriek that left the group clapping their hands over their ears. Their faces twisted as their hands grew sharp claws, teeth gave way to fangs, and their eyes rolled back in their skulls. It was clear they were corrupted, enslaved to the will of Vulcan. At once, they rushed towards the group in a frenzy of deadly, swinging and clawing swipes.

The first line of corrupted were met with a broad smash from Drogon's heavy shield – splattering four faces with a single thrust. He pushed into them with a spin that focused a series of pummels and slashes. His movements were cleverly calculated to leave no part of him exposed. As he would batter in one direction, he would offset his balance with a stab in the other. He cut slowly through the mass of corrupted. He was moving to support Stein, who had separated himself from the group.

Marlow howled with excitement. The fur on the back of his neck stood on end and his face was untamed and bestial. His eyes gleamed with rage, showing nothing but bloodlust. He heaved his great axe wildly in wide arcs that cleaved through several corrupted with each broad, bloody stroke. They were cut at the neck, the gut, or the torso—but always into two pieces. He continued forward, tossing the blade from side to side with little effort, as if he was harvesting grain.

Tholden grinned, "Seventy or seven hundred, all corrupted fall before Tholden Moonstorm!" He raised his hands over his head, concentrating the fire in his palms to fill the air above him into a pillar of flame. The pillar then started to spin and created a vortex that crested upward, scorching the ceiling. "Burn baby," he said softly as he dropped his palms out in front of him. The vortex followed and engulfed the corrupted in his path. They ignited like kindling and collapsed almost instantly into a burnt pile of bones.

The human vetaless stood at the end of his seared path of corpses. She hissed and sprinted straight towards him with unnatural speed.

He stood poised and held out one hand with his index and middle fingers extended. With his other hand, he supported his wrist and squinted one eye to line up his shot, "something special for you, love," he said to himself.

From his fingers, a small red jolt shot with lightning speed. It left a trail of energy lingering in the air that slowly fell like dust with smoke rising off his fingertips. The trail followed from his hand straight through the vetaless heart and out her back, taking out a corrupted behind her. She had been moving with such speed that her body gave way to a forward slide and left her face inches from Tholden's boot.

Grekk had only a short sword stowed beneath his elegant garb. He positioned himself side to side with Garf, who was wielding his worn dagger. Their eyes met for a moment and Grekk's raspy voice shouted, "I wish I brought something bigger. Let's do this!"

"Aye," replied Garf.

The two accomplished a display of footwork, maneuvering in figure eights to one another. Garf kicked one noble in the gut, and with his free hand grabbed another by the throat and pierced the dagger into his temple. Without hesitation, he withdrew the blade, and tossed the corpse at another that was advancing towards Grekk. With a quick step, he buried the dagger to the hilt through the skull of yet another. In the close encounters with the corrupted, Garf was being scratched and ripped by the claws of the creatures. His skin was peeling from his forearms. Blood was rushing over his hands, spraying crimson drips over the marble floors.

Lee stood three feet behind Garf and held both his hands out before him, "I can help. Hang in there, Garf!" From his hands the green healing current rushed, spiraling and illuminating as it encapsulated his friend. It warmed Garf's entire body with a soft, soothing sensation. Garf could see blood streaming back up his hands and into his body while fighting on. The shreds of flesh begun folding back over themselves and pulling rips and tears of the wounds together. He was amazed and empowered. Lee kept channeling the energy into him, mending gashes almost as quickly as Garf could suffer them.

Grekk unleashed a flurry of swipes with his short sword, dancing between Garf's kicks and playing to opportunity. With his superior perception, he noticed the elf vetaless hurrying forward - ducking behind the noble-creatures and leaving Garf blind to the advancing threat. Grekk shifted, ducking under a falling corrupted and rolling it off his back. He used the momentum and slid on his knees, arcing back his neck to glide between the legs of another. As he cleared, he thrust himself upward and forward towards the vetaless blade first.

His impressive tactics to surprise the elf were unrewarded. As soon as he leapt up to attack, the vetaless locked eyes with him. She saw him coming and positioned herself to catch him before he regained his footing. As he reached out with his blade, she effortlessly shrugged back her shoulder, missing her by a hairsbreadth. In the same motion, she grabbed his arm and yanked him into her. Her face lunged forward, her fangs ripping into the scales of his neck. She quickly tore out a chunk of his throat. Blood spurted over the dance floor as Grekk dropped his sword and crumbled to the ground. He frantically grabbed at his wound, trying to cover a hole larger than both his hands. He writhed about, as the floor was stained red. Blood spat from his mouth as he shouted, "I'm dying!"

Lee's eyes widened in horror, "Oh no, Grekk! Garf, we have to help him! I'm right behind you, go that way."

"You got it, Scrap." Garf began pushing forward into the mass, taking down corrupted after corrupted, but making very slow progress. He was slashed and bitten over and over, but Lee was skilled enough to heal him just as fast. As Garf was nearing

Grekk, the remaining vetaless found her way between them.

"Come to die with him?" She threatened, stepping closer.

Garf answered the rhetorical question, "No, I've come to help him."

He lunged at her, catching her wrist in one hand and driving his dagger towards her face with the other. She caught his arm, and the two spun wildly, wrestling with claw and dagger. She dug into his wrist with her bloody claw as they struggled until Garf snarled with pain and was toppled back. The elven vetaless continued chomping at him as their arms fought for a better hold.

Garf slipped and fell on his back; the vetaless pinned him down and buried her claws into the bone of his arm. Her hot, fetid breath filled his nostrils as her teeth grazed his face. His muscles fatigued and started to give out. "Lee," he shouted, "get to Tholden."

"I won't leave you," Lee said. He had narrowly dodged the grasp of a corrupted and continued his focus on healing Garf.

"Now!" he ordered.

Lee hesitated, not wanting to leave his friend, stopped his healing, and quickly turned away.

Garf thrashed about as the jaws of the vetaless began scraping layers of skin from his cheek. He felt his arm giving way as his dagger was pressed to the floor. He took a deep breath, closed his eyes, and gave the last bit of strength he had to hold her off for a final second.

When Garf accepted his fate of not seeing another sunrise—suddenly her grip loosened. Garf opened his eyes to see her over him, her mouth hanging open, eyes going blank, and blood spilling from her lips. As she leaned back, he saw Grekk's sword had pierced through her chest. Behind her stood young Lee, his two hands grasping the hilt and tears strolling down his face.

Garf threw the dead elf off and stood up. Putting a hand on Lee's shoulder he said, "You saved my life, Scrap."

Lee was crying and staring down at the vetaless, "I've never killed anyone." He turned away almost as quickly as he said it and rushed toward Grekk. By the time he reached him, Grekk was no longer moving. His body lay limp and scales flushed. Lee laid both hands over the hole in his neck. "Please," he pleaded. A rush of energy passed into Grekk, creating ripples in the puddle of blood that was surrounding them. "Come on!" He focused harder, splattering the puddle. The wound wouldn't mend. Lee sat weeping as Garf and Tholden stood protectively over him.

As the party had taken on the corrupted and the vetaless, Stein had engaged the vetala lord – Vulcan. His first attack had left him only inches from the towering vetala, but he did not cower. Vulcan retaliated with a swipe from his monstrous claw, narrowly missing his chest and tearing away at his freshly pressed robes. Stein rebalanced himself. Spinning the scythe from bottom to top, he sliced into the marble of the floor and followed the blade back up towards the monster's face. It was a near miss—close enough for the intense flame to scorch the vetala's skin. Vulcan seized the opening and brought down a massive fist from overhead. The force of the blow brought Stein to his knees.

"You are nothing. I will consume you as I have countless before you," Vulcan boasted. "You look comfortable on your knees. Your pitiful gods must love you."

Stein said nothing, spat blood from his mouth, and rolled forward. He slid the crooked blade between the vetala's feet and hooked into his calf. He spun in place and with a powerful heave, buried the weapon deep into the bone and pulled his foot out from under him. Vulcan was thrown to the ground with a howl. Stein swung back his blade and cleaved it forward into Vulcan's leg again, attempting to sever it. The slice was clean, but the thick, monstrous bone held the blade in place. Stein heaved with all his might, trying to force the blade with a mighty thrust.

Before he could break through, Vulcan pried the scythe free, tumbling Stein backwards onto the floor. Vulcan leaned towards him, setting free a savage barrage of swipes. Stein dodged and blocked, but was slashed over and over. His attacks were relentless, and Stein was on the defensive while being forced back, even further from his allies.

The intensity of Stein's start pierced into Vulcan. He was fast but predictable. After the second series repeated, he found a pattern. Stein ducked under the first claw, whirled around the second and with a masterful spin of his weapon, pierced the flaming blade through Vulcan's chest. Stein appreciated the moment. Inch by inch, he savored the cracking of ribs and crunching of flesh until he felt the resistance release from the exit wound. Stein inhaled slowly, relishing the moment.

Vulcan moaned in shock, "this can't b-" as he fell to his knees. His black eyes once filled with anger and hatred began to fill with fear.

Stein stood before him, staring into his eyes. He didn't blink or show any emotion, even as Vulcan coughed blood over his face He watched as the unnatural life left him. It wasn't until the complete essence of energy had left him that Stein pulled the blade from his chest and allowed the body to collapse onto the floor.

It was at this moment that the last remaining lords and ladies collapsed to the floor and returned to their normal state; released from Vulcan's magic. The violent sounds of battle immediately fell away. An eerie silence filled the great hall. The group had slain nearly all the seventy corrupted, leaving only a handful to be released of the vetala's hold.

There was a stillness in the great hall as the party realized that many innocent lives were lost here tonight. They exchanged looks of confusion and shock. At both the carnage surrounding them, and that they still stood.

Drogon stood beside Stein and sheathed his sword. "Is-is everyone all right?"

"No," Lee cried out, "Grekk is dead, I couldn't save him."

Drogon walked over and laid his hands upon Grekk. Another warm green energy passed through him and it, and like Lee's attempts, had no effect. Drogon reached over and closed Grekk's eyes, "There was nothing you could do."

"I couldn't do anything," Lee said, "I couldn't get to him. I couldn't heal him."

"No, you couldn't," Drogon said, "and you may not always be able to. We will talk later. For now, we must go. Marlow please carry Grekk – we are taking him with us."

Marlow stowed his axe and lifted Grekk with great care.

The party walked through the main hall, out the front door, and down the steps of the mansion to the waiting carriage. Marlow and Drogon climbed atop and with a whip, Constantine and Dash were off to the barn. The streets were quiet, save for an armed patrol that was heading to investigate the scene of the party.

Stein put his arm over Lee and pulled him close. Everyone was covered in blood, black and red – but none more than young Lee. His three-piece suit was smeared from top to bottom and he was lost within himself. He peered down at the black goo of his first kill, and the red vitality of his fallen friend. He briefly remembered his excitement for this party and now felt nothing but regret. After all, when he got into the carriage earlier, it still had the faint smell of pancakes and syrup. Now – there was only the coppery scent of blood and death.

The tears left streams of visible skin where the blood was washed away, "*I* am the monster." he mumbled.

VI

<u>No Good Deed</u>

*"In this place you will find neither hope nor light. No –
in this place there is only the shadow of my will with the
force of my vengeance."*
The Black Book – A Tribute to Amon.

The barn doors had been locked down tight and tonight—no lanterns were lit. The carriage, along with Constantine and Dash, were hidden inside. Drogon kept a constant patrol around the perimeter to watch the town's lanterns spring to life in the distance.

Lee could no longer tell if it was late or early. From the group, there was no snoring or restful breathing. Everyone was lying in the darkness of the barn, silent with their heavy thoughts. His eyes darted between the pile of hay where Grekk would sleep and the carriage—where his remains were kept. There was a great weight in Lee's heart, a feeling of regret and of failure.

Stein's voice carried from the hay bale above, "Lee?"

"I'm awake," his voice trailed.

"I'm proud of you."

"Why? I killed Grekk, I couldn't save him." Lee cried.

"No, the vetaless killed Grekk and you avenged him. You saved Garf's life in the process too," Stein said.

"That you did," said Garf from the darkness.

Lee said, "Hi, Garf."

Stein continued, "There are not many that could do as you did. By stopping Vulcan, we stopped him from feeding off the rest of the city. You saved Tristian tonight."

"But I couldn't save Grekk!" he cried, "or that poor elven woman I killed. My dad said the curse would be unbreakable, but as soon as you stopped Vulcan they changed back. That means I killed her - we could've saved them all."

"She wasn't just an elf when she was attacking Grekk and Garf; she was a monster. Even if we had to kill every last one of them to stop him - we would still be doing the town and the world a favor," Stein said with confidence, "you did the right thing."

"It doesn't feel that way," said Lee.

Stein reached down his hand and rested it softly on Lee's head, "It won't come easy for you. Believe me, that's a good thing. What if we make a pact – you and me?"

Lee rolled over to look up at him atop the hay bale. In the darkness, he could see only the silhouette of Stein's face peering over several feet above him. He could see the gleam of his eyes, "What do you mean?"

"I don't want to see you this way. If you can find the strength to forgive yourself and accept that what you did was necessary; you will never have to kill anyone again." Stein reached out his hand to shake on it.

Lee lied still, "But there will always be something we're after, right? What if I *had to*?"

"You won't, because I promise to kill it for you," he said coldly. "Anything that threatens you or that needs to die; I will kill it. I think it's a good thing that this is so hard on you, but it can't keep you down forever. I don't have the same problem. Killing is easy for me - always has been. We can play off each other's strengths; it will be good for both of us."

He took a deep breath, "Okay, Stein," he shook his hand, "I promise."

Stein laid back down and out of view. Lee could already feel a weight lift off of him from Stein's promise. He finally closed his eyes and fell asleep.

As his soft snore began, much of the tension in the barn was relieved. Soon after, Garf and Marlow began snoozing away. Between the three of them, one could no longer hear the shuffling of Drogon's boots through the hay.

It was as Stein was about to close his eyes that Tholden's whisper beckoned to him, "Stein?"

"What, Tholden?" Stein's tone was filled with frustration.

"What is it with you and this kid? You're not nice to anyone, so why the soft spot?" he asked.

"He's a good kid. I want him to stay that way."

"There's more to it than that, isn't there? Does he remind you of one of your brothers? Let's see, the royal family has three sons; Victus, Bradley and then yourself. Or maybe he reminds you of yourself? I know there's more than what you're telling me. You aren't even this thoughtful towards me and I've been traveling with you for months."

Stein let out a long sigh.

"Just tell me," Tholden begged.

"It's because I don't like you, Tholden," Stein replied and rolled onto his side.

Drogon approached Tholden from the shadows, unnoticed, and bumped his ribs with his boot, "Leave him be, Tholden. He doesn't need to feed your quest for knowledge – or gossip."

"Yes, yes," Tholden said, "good night, then."

There were only a few hours of rest until the sun began to light up the barn. Almost all at once, everyone sat up in their bedding and greeted one another with groggy stares. There was a faint smell of smoke and ash in the air. Drogon was near the wall; where he shifted a loose board aside and stuck him arm through.

Lee approached him, "What are you doing?"

"I am waiting to hear from our scout," he replied.

"We have scouts? This must be quite a big group you have," Lee said.

There was a rustling outside by Drogon's arm, "Here he is now." He pulled his arm back in and sitting upon his forearm was a small **dragonling**. It was no taller than an average housecat and covered in purple scales that were slightly more vibrant than Drogon's red scales. The dragonling arched back his neck and eagerly accepted the petting and adoration from his master. "Lee, meet Argon. Argon, this is Lee, he is our friend."

"Hello Argon, it is nice to meet you." Lee held out his hand to pet him.

Argon tilted his head and looked to Drogon for approval. Drogon nodded and at once Argon ran up young Lee's arm and sat upon his shoulder, nudging his head and chewing on his hair.

Lee giggled excitedly, "I like you too!"

"You two can get to know each other later, but we have work to do first." Drogon whistled and Argon flew back to his arm, "What did you see?" he asked the small dragonling.

The dragonling began making a series of mystifying snarls and growls that were clearly understood by Drogon. He snarled back and seemed to probe for more information. Lee stood confused, but continued to watch their unusual conversation.

Tholden walked over to look on with Lee, "They are speaking **draconic** or **dragon tongue**. It is an ancient language of the earliest dragons. Are you familiar with it?"

"No. I never knew any dragonkin before Drogon," Lee replied.

"It's truly fascinating to hear a dragon speak. It is argued to be the eldest language, but many masters believe elven came first," Tholden added.

"Do you know what they're saying?" Lee asked.

Tholden scoffed, "I speak many languages, mind you. Let's see, Drogon is asking how big of an army is marching. Argon says there are two hundred and they're being led Prince Victus and General Dart."

Drogon shot Tholden a warning look that said, "Stop."

Tholden stopped speaking at once and shook Lee's shoulder, "I'm sure if it's important we will know soon enough." He turned, placed his hand on Lee's back, and led him towards the improvised table, "Let's start with breakfast."

As the group gathered around the table, Tholden sparked the air to arrange plates and bowls with cutlery and drinking glasses at each setting. In another flash of orange light, the glasses filled with water and the dishes with oats and sliced fruits. Everyone sat and began eating in silence as Drogon and Argon continued their conversation by the door. After several minutes, Argon flew atop a rafter while Drogon came to join them.

Drogon began eating at his fruit as the party stared at him.

"Well?" said Lee.

Drogon took one bite, swallowed, and said, "It's difficult to say. It is either very bad or it's nothing at all."

Garf laughed, "Can we finish our breakfast or should we head for the hills?"

Drogon's face became stern. "Prince Victus is marching a company here to Tristian."

A silence fell over the group.

"Why would he be leading soldiers here? We're the only army he needs," Marlow said.

"Maybe they plan to defend from an invasion of the **Vian Kingdom** that we aren't aware of – we're overdue for another war with them," Tholden said.

"Tristian isn't really on the way," Stein added, "and my father wouldn't risk his heir defending from an invasion."

"I agree. I think it is much simpler than that," said Drogon, "we haven't reported back to General Dart since we liberated Sundale from the hydra. I believe they are sending troops to hunt down the vetala under the presumption we failed."

"Two hundred for a vetala?" Tholden argued.

"Think of it like this - how many soldiers would it take to stop a creature that could stand up to *us*?" Drogon said.

The group looked at each other and agreed confidently. They knew they were formidable.

"Of course, there is another possibility," Drogon looked toward Stein, "If they know you are with us, they will come for you."

Stein leaned back in his chair, "That would explain Victus coming to 'collect' me."

"We won't let him!" Lee shouted. "You have to stay here with us, we're family."

Tholden said, "Victus is his *actual* family, and I don't think all of us should be willing to fight against two hundred Radiant Empire soldiers so that Stein could keep up as runaway prince at our expense."

Lee slapped the table, "They did terrible experiments on him and we can't let them take him! If you think what they did is okay, why don't we let them chop you up and see if you like it?"

The party stared at Lee in surprise.

"We don't know if that's why they're here," Drogon added, "this could go one of two ways so we will be sure to leave ourselves a backup plan. I think we should split up to make sure this goes smoothly."

"I'm with Stein," Lee said.

"I couldn't agree more. Stein, Lee, and Marlow will go to the docks with the rest of our coin. We need a ship and crew that can get us to the city of **Rayton** with all the necessary provisions."

"Why Rayton?" Garf said.

"I have family there. Stein could lie low with them in the event they have caught onto him. And if it's nothing, we will set sail elsewhere and wait for new orders. I just want to be prepared for the worst. Keep in mind, if this does go south, we will need that ship ready very soon, understood?"

"Get a ship. Got it," said Marlow.

"And what about me?" asked Garf.

"Garf, Tholden and I will go greet Victus and his company when they arrive at the gates. We will tell them about our slaying of the vetala and find out what they are doing here. I will bring Grekk's remains so they can be taken back for a proper burial," Drogon said. "If they know about you, Stein, I will tell them you ran off when you caught word of their march."

Garf was wearing a nervous look, "Do I have to go with you?"

"They're *our* soldiers, Garf. Our allies," Tholden laughed, "and our own government wouldn't bring harm to us. Besides, General Dart can pay our reward and we can sail off to Rayton to see Drogon's mother."

"How did you know it was my mother in Rayton?" Drogon said.

Tholden laughed, "I just thought of the saddest place to have to hideout and knew it had to involve a tiny house with your mother."

Drogon said, "If everyone is ready, I would like to get on with it."

The party stood from the table and separated. They began to gather all of their things scattered from about the barn. It was only a few minutes until there was no trace of a weeklong campout.

Drogon, Garf, and Tholden sat atop the carriage and rolled towards the **west gate** at the end of Mantis Lane. It was unusual for them to have an arrival of empire forces in Tristian. It was even more so unusual that these forces were being led by the heir to the throne. They continued calmly, but remained ready for whatever was going to happen.

Elsewhere; Marlow, Stein, and Lee loaded up their gear and the last of the coin in their backpacks. They walked at a quickened pace for the docks. All the while walking, Lee was wondering exactly how they were going to get a ship until at last he asked, "Can you just buy a ship like that? Isn't there paperwork or something involved?"

Stein didn't break his pace, "Normally there would be, but in our case—we can skip that part."

"How though?" said Lee.

"I am going to offer them gold for their ship so we can sail off free and clear. We'll deal with the port documents later. Some captains might view this as *sketchy*. If that's the case, we'd have to either move onto a different ship or simply take it."

"Take it?"

Stein replied, "Our need is greater. I will relieve someone of their ship if the need calls for it."

"They won't just let you have it, though." said Lee with an innocent concern for the plan's success.

"Then I will relieve them of their life."

#

<u>Fight and Flight</u>

*"There is no real charity – things are only given
freely through fear, obligation, or guilt. We are selfish,
the ones who accept this will always have more."*
Confessions of the Temptress – A Tribute to Eve.

Every street to the north of Mantis Lane was being patrolled by armed guards. There was smoke rising up from what the three could recognize as the Path of Rubies and it was accompanied by the smell of burning meat.

Tholden had to yell over the gallop of the horses, "You think they're burning bodies?"

"Probably," Drogon replied, "the guards don't know anything about vetala lore. It's the safe approach. I'm more concerned why there are so many patrolmen around."

"The corrupted turned back into nobles when Vulcan was killed. I'm sure it looks more like massacre than the extermination it was." Tholden explained.

Drogon nodded, "You're probably right Best avoid the patrols as much as possible."

"I couldn't agree more."

Drogon chose a detour and directed Dash and Constantine to hurry the carriage through the south streets of the commons. Here it seemed the people were conducting business as usual, but on closer inspection, many were whispering back and forth to one another. They were quickly able to leave the area and arrived at the west gate.

At one time, the town of Tristian had been surrounded by a mighty thirty-foot stonewall. Over the decades, as war and time collapsed it away, a stout fifteen-footwall remained. The west gate was the last structure remaining of original height and it towered over the surrounding wall. As usual in Tristian in these times, the gate was open and many a traveler was passing in and out. They stopped and left the horses and carriage within the walls. The three then walked through the gate and stood outside.

"Did Argon have any idea why they were coming?" Garf asked.

"He doesn't understand common tongue," Drogon said, "he can only scout and report."

Tholden said with a smirk, "That doesn't seem very useful now does it?"

"I'd rather have this little bit of information versus nothing at all," Drogon replied.

"That's comical, Drogon, because I feel like that's exactly what we have—nothing at all," he paused for a moment. "We don't know if they're coming here to kill us or reward us, but here we are; standing at the gates."

"They would only be looking to kill Stein. We aren't in any danger," Drogon said.

Tholden raised his voice, "You think if the Radiant Empire found out we recruited Stein into our party and hid him from them that they would let us walk—free and clear?"

Garf looked to Drogon with his face flushed with doubt, "Yeah, that's true. Why wouldn't they kill us too?"

"We have done a lot in the name of the empire and the royal family over the decade; that doesn't go forgotten. General Dart is with them, as well, and he would never let anything like that happen," Drogon said with confidence, "all that we've done for them is worth something."

"You're a fool," Tholden said, "as are all paladins, in fact. You hold yourself to be so righteous and honorable, but you misplace your trust. You think the world is as kind and true? You think you are? You're wrong."

"What do you know about being righteous or honorable?" Drogon asked.

"That it isn't worth any more than the coins I make out of rock and bits of wood. You don't truly believe that we are valuable to the empire, do you? We are only worth whatever we've done for them lately. I would doubt they even remember Sundale." Tholden mumbled.

"Maybe not, but today we give them Tristian," said Drogon.

"Hopefully we can keep saving cities every day then," Tholden laughed, "you're insufferable."

Garf moved between them, "Oye, Tholden, it's Drogon you're talking about and where he stands; so do I—and so should you."

"You're wrong," he repeated timidly as he turned back to lean against the wall.

Drogon was unmoved by Tholden's words.

The three stood in silence and continued to wait outside the gates. It was approaching the early evening when they finally heard the rumble of the footsteps and saw two hundred gleaming soldiers approaching Tristian. They were wearing the polished chrome armor typical of the Radiant Empire and were being led by two men on horseback.

The first was a broad human with a shined scalp and rosy cheeks. He was a Radiant General and his blue uniform was decorated with an impressive display of medals. This bald brute was General Dart, as Argon mentioned. He sat on his horse, erect and without expression.

The second man they recognized as Prince Victus—heir to the Radiant Empire. He was as pale and lean as Stein, with the similar tribal markings on his face and neck. He had long blonde hair that fell to the middle of his back and wore no uniform, but rather an ornate leather armor reinforced with the same chrome plating. He also sat erect and without expression.

Drogon, Tholden, and Garf bowed towards the prince and moved up slowly. Victus and Dart dropped from their horses and approached them. They wore no expression on their faces and moved with rigidity.

"You alright?" Garf asked Dart. "You don't look good."

Tholden stood behind his allies and whispered to Drogon, "Something isn't right, I don't like this."

"You are to throw down your weapons at once and come with us," Dart ordered, grasping the hilt of his sword.

"General, what is the meaning of this? We have done nothing wrong," said Drogon.

"The Radiant Empire commands your obedience and service. I am ordering you to relinquish your weapons," he repeated.

Drogon remained motionless before he spoke, "We are willing to cooperate, but tell us what is going on."

"You will be escorted to the king and he will tell you himself," said Dart.

"Will you guarantee our safe return?" Tholden slipped in.

Dart looked to him assuredly, "You will not be harmed. I need you only to hand over your weapons."

A soldier stepped forward with his arms out, "Give it here."

Drogon parted with his sword and gestured to the others to do the same. Garf surrendered his three short swords and four daggers. Tholden, though not needing of a weapon to cast, gave a wand for good measure.

The sea of soldiers parted to reveal a throne at the rear of the column of soldiers. It was being carried by a dozen exhausted elves who were dressed in elegant clothing. Victus and Dart led the group back towards the throne and as they approached, they were met with a most terrifying sight.

The party witnessed the throne carrying not the king—but a familiar figure. A human with purple eyes and jet-black hair who wore blue and gold ordained robes. He sat in a pose of arrogance with a sinister grin spreading from ear to ear.

Drogon's mouth hung open is disbelief.

Tholden keeled back in shock.

Garf looked on in confusion—not recognizing who the man was.

"Donahay," Drogon said.

"That's impossible!" gasped Tholden.

"Why is he sitting on a throne?" Garf asked innocently.

Drogon whispered back to him, "He is a demigod. We encountered him in Sundale. Whatever you do, don't look into his eyes, Garf, *your* mind would be easy to control."

"Aye," he obeyed.

"Drogon, Tholden, is that you?" said the ominous figure perched on his throne. "Oh my, it has been a while since I've seen you two. Where are the others? Where is Grekk—I'd like to thank him," he stood from the throne and started towards them, "who is that one with you?"

"How did you escape?" Tholden said in a higher pitch than usual, "you were locked in the **magestry**."

"How did I escape, are you being witty again Tholden? You couldn't have thought your *professors* and *lawmakers* could possibly possess the knowledge to keep me sealed away—no. That would be insulting if you really believe that was the case."

"Then how did you do it?" Drogon insisted.

Donahay looked around, searching for someone. "Well, that is why I asked you for Grekk, where is he?"

Garf's eyes were fixed to the ground. "He's dead."

Donahay continued moving towards them, "That's a pity; he was an inquisitive one—so curious. He had so many questions about magic, and my master plan, that he actually came to the magestry to interrogate me some time ago. Being bound, gagged, suspended and blindfolded left any visitor one, which I would entertain. He got so caught up in the knowledge I shared with him—that when he left, he forgot to muzzle me again. Needless to say, all I needed was to utter an incantation and my slaver set me free." He now stood only a few feet from them, "who is this half-breed with you?"

Garf kept his head down, staring at his feet, "The name's Garf, of Clan Unkle."

"Ah, and I suppose our friends here have told you about me? No matter, the three of you are of little threat to me with the army that stands at my back. I have no need to kill you. Although, if I'm being honest, which I always am; I haven't decided just yet if I will or not."

Drogon positioned himself in front of Garf, "What have you done with King Treyalt?"

Donahay laughed, "You are worrying about Treyalt right now? I would have thought you would be more concerned with your own situation." He gestured to the army surrounding them.

"He's a paladin," sighed Tholden.

"Right," Donahay agreed, "insufferable."

Tholden was amused, "Tell me about it."

Drogon shot Tholden a silencing look and turned back towards Donahay, "What of the king?"

"He is currently managing my affairs back at the **Radiant Castle**. I left him to handle recruitment, organizing, and forging the weapons for our great conquest. You see, Drogon," he rested his hand on Drogon's shoulder, "I have infiltrated the minds of the entire capital. Your magestry sits at the very heart of the empire. Once I was set free, I had only to dominate the few in charge to have them and funnel the masses to me. While the rest of my forces mobilize, I thought it best to visit my outlying cities, like Tristian, here. After all, I can't lead the Radiant Empire to unite the world if we ourselves aren't under one mind. The entire northern continent is mine already, it won't be long now."

The party was silent.

Donahay said, "I'm telling you this, because I believe I have finally made up my mind on what to do with you."

Drogon was analyzing the soldiers around them. At a closer look, he could see all of them had a purple glaze over their eyes—showing a form of mind control. He spotted the soldier carrying their gear looking on, no more than fifteen feet away.

Tholden spoke hurriedly, "Perhaps you have need of an advisor?"

Garf and Drogon turned to Tholden in shock.

Tholden continued, "Someone whose mind is freed, but also fluent in the magical arts and warfare? I might be one such sorcerer."

"No," Drogon asserted. "None of us will join you. We won't let you hold the empire to your madness."

"Speak for yourself, Drogon." Tholden looked to Donahay, "I would rather join you."

Donahay burst into a maniacal laughter and stepped closer to them, "Drogon, you inspire no loyalty in your men, do you? I'm not surprised!" He stood inches from Tholden and his face abruptly tightening into a calculating stare, "Or maybe you are as spineless as you look." He sniffed the air, "Yes, you reek of cowardice, Tholden. I despise a mage who has no morals. Me? I am a dark mage – I am openly in it for myself. You? You hide beneath a veil of false confidence and behind the shield of your so-claimed allies. In reality, you are fodder. My legacy is being built on the corpses of men like you. No offense."

Tholden's hands trembled as he mumbled, "That's purely offensive."

"Don't be upset, you swine. Drogon will probably still keep you around since he's such a quality guy. In fact—listen to this," he turned towards Drogon, "how about it Drogon, will you be my advisor?"

"Never." His snout twitched as he spoke.

"See—now that makes me want you even more."

Donahay stared into Drogon's eyes. A powerful purple light beamed through the air and Drogon stumbled back. For an instant, Drogon's eyes were glazed over with the same purple hue. He stared expressionless for a moment—only—a moment. Then, he mustered the will to shake his head fiercely and at once, it faded away.

"Damn," said Donahay, "perhaps it's best if I just kill you."

Garf stood with his feet spaced apart and his arms in a defensive stance. Even he could discern that a spell, which could nearly dominate Drogon, would certainly overtake him. He closed his eyes and stood, ready to fight blind.

Drogon regained his footing and caught his breath. His eyes focused with ferocity onto Donahay. "Let me make this easy for you." He held his hand up over his head and shouted, "Rayne, come!"

The soldier carrying their gear rushed forward in a jerky stumbling move, pulled by the weapons themselves. He fell forward and they were scattered to the ground, except for Drogon's sword, Rayne. The sword flew through the air with precision and was guided directly into Drogon's readied hand.

"Fine with me. Go on, get them!" Donahay commanded while scurrying back towards his throne.

In the same motion which he had caught the hilt, Drogon brought down the sword through the helm of the nearest soldier. He jumped forward towards the pile of weapons and nimbly dodged the wild slashing of the mindless troops. With the weapons at his feet, he spun in a perfect whirlwind of stabs and parries. When at last he was not immediately surrounded, he reached down for Garf's short swords, "Garf!" He shouted as he threw them, "Open your eyes."

Garf was grappling at the soldiers with his eyes shut tight. He was already riddled with cuts and two arrows stuck from his back. Upon hearing Drogon's words, he instantly obeyed, locking his eyes onto the airborne blades. He stepped forward, heaving a hard kick into the breast of an axe man, reaching up to collect his weapons. As the familiar hilt of his ax met his palm as he leapt back, dodging a blade and retaliating with a nasty backswing. He buried the blade into the soldier and struggled to pry it out of his chest.

Drogon reached down again, collecting Tholden's wand. He turned to throw it and shouted, "Tholden!" but stopped, speechless. As his eyes fixed in the distance, he could see a blip, the spark of a spell, teleporting Tholden past the soldiers and towards the city. "Tholden!" The rage in his voice erupted over the sounds of battle. As Tholden disappeared into the streets, the wand itself blipped away and Drogon's hand hung empty.

Garf was overwhelmed. Blood soaked his armor and he was beginning to feel sluggish from the now six arrows protruding from his back and chest. "Drogon," he cried.

Drogon whipped back his shield as an arrow met his shoulder. He held it out in front of him and raged forward towards Garf, toppling a straight path of soldiers. The two stood back to back, under constant siege from every side. Drogon shifted back his shield to cover Garf from ranged fire while Garf parried enemies around Drogon's block. Together, they rotated with their attacks and slowly worked their way back towards the city gate.

While the battle was raging on, it was fiercer than a lesser warrior could endure. Garf was leaving a trail of blood and his swings were losing strength. In a powerful thrust, the pike of a soldier broke through Garf's block and cut deep into his gut. He collapsed forward onto his knees and let out a tired moan. Another attacker followed up and Garf was met with a sword piercing into his shoulder.

Drogon parried quickly and sliced down, breaking the pike blade from the shaft. He threw *Rayne* to the ground and pivoted his shield to his sword arm, allowing him to hoist Garf over his shoulder. He charged through the last few enemies to break through at a full sprint towards the gate.

A stampede of the soldiers' boots and clanging armor sounded behind them.

"Drogon, I'm done," Garf coughed blood from his mouth, "put me down and get outta here."

"Save your breath, you're going to make it," he said. "Rayne, come." And the blade was summoned back to its sheath.

"I got a pike in my lung," Garf said, "I'm slowing you down."

The whistle of an arrow fell silent as it pierced Drogon's back plate. He didn't lose pace. "Where you fall, so do I—and it won't be here."

They had crossed the threshold of the gate and were back in Tristian. Drogon heaved Garf atop the carriage and whipped Dash and Constantine into a full gallop. He gripped the reins in one hand, and with the other hand focused a green hue of healing magical light over Garf's chest. The blood flowing from his wounds slowed, but they only partially mended. Garf blacked out.

Drogon landed a smack across his face, "Stay with me!"

The carriage raced across the commons scattering citizens from the roads. Behind them, Drogon heard the Radiant forces ransacking homes and herding the people into the streets. Donahay strolled in with his chrome-wearing escorts through the west gate and greeted every terrified citizen personally with a warm smile. As they would meet his gaze, they would stiffen beside him; under his full control.

After a few frantic minutes, they arrived at the docks. Drogon jumped off scanning the piers, looking for any sign of his allies. At last, he saw the broad horns of Marlow aboard a ship with *Yoshi* painted on the bow. It appeared ill maintained and was dwarfed by the other vessels in port. Drogon lifted Garf off the seat, but could feel he was no longer breathing. Frantically ripping open the door, he pulled Grekk's body from the carriage and ran towards the ship with his comrades draped over his shoulders.

Stein, Lee, and Marlow heard the clatter of boots racing across the pier.

"Stein, Drogon's back—looks like they're in trouble," Lee said with shrill panic in his voice.

Stein looked out into the port and without hesitation leapt over the rail and down to the pier and dashed towards Drogon. He lifted Garf from Drogon's shoulder without breaking stride, "What happened?"

"Donahay," Drogon replied.

His face was bitter with enraging surprise, "Where's Tholden?"

Drogon was panting—his wounds taking their toll. "He tried to join Donahay. Then shame got the better of him and he ran off when they wouldn't have him."

Stein peered to Drogon, at first with a look of confusion and then with rage, "He's dead."

"He might have been trying to-" Drogon was cut short.

"No," Stein protested, "he's dead *when* we find him."

They ran back up the ramp and laid their allies on deck.

Stein laid Garf down gently and announced to the party, "Tholden is mine. If anyone sees him, tell me right away."

Lee focused his mind and positioned himself over Garf. His entire body radiated a strong green glow, running up through his chest and funneling down to his palms. It was pulsing out over Garf and wrapped around his body. Garf didn't move. His wounds didn't mend. "Garf!" Lee cried.

His eyes shut hard and tightened as he grit his teeth, straining his focus. The glow surged, pushing forward faster, brighter, and with an intensity that swayed Lee's robes like a stormy wind. He felt his body loosen as he fell forward with a gasp.

Stein rested both his hands on Lee's shoulders, "It's okay, Lee. You've done what you could."

"No, no, it's not okay. I couldn't save him—I couldn't help," Lee said.

Drogon hung his head. "It's my fault; I didn't make it in time."

"There's one other thing I could try! I've seen my father do it a few times," Lee threw down his pack and quickly searched through, "I'm not going to let you die, Garf. I can help." Tears were streaming down his face as he pulled out the bundles of heartbane, cocoon silk and the trace bit of phoenix dust, and sky spark. He began grinding them down and crushing them into dust. He held his hands out over the mixture and focused all of his energy. The vibrant green light was running through him. He felt a vibration in his chest and heard a soft hum in his ears. Suddenly, his body shivered with an icy chill and his head became too heavy to hold up. Lee began to sway and the all sound faded away around him.

He fell to his side, eyes rolled back, and collapsed limply on the ground.

VIII

Stowaway

*"If there is only one world to pioneer, be sure to have
set your feet upon every soil and bathe in every sea."
Claiming the Heavens – A Tribute to Hosridon.*

Lee woke up feeling the gentle rocking of the ship at sea. He was below deck in a small cabin furnished only with a bed and small desk. There was a rusty oil lantern hanging beside the door that rubbed back and forth against the wood in a soothing rhythm. From outside, he heard a faint crunching sound. As soon as he sat up, the noise stopped and the door creaked open.

Stein entered taking the last bite from an apple, "You're up?"

"What happened to me?" Lee asked.

"Your heart stopped while you were trying to make something. It took all of Drogon's strength to stabilize you," Stein explained. "I know you want to help, but you can't take risks like that, okay?"

"But I do—I just wanted to help. I wasn't going to let another friend die. I will give everything I have," Lee said.

Stein sat next to him, "I know, but don't kill yourself in the process next time," he said, "it was brave what you did, I'm proud of you."

Lee smiled, "Thanks, Stein. What happened to Garf?"

"You made, Drogon called it, a seed of life. Unfortunately, it didn't work the way we hoped. The good thing is that Garf is breathing, but hasn't woken up. Don't worry, from what Drogon said, it takes decades to master something like that—even for a talented cleric like you. It's incredible that you were able to stabilize him, at all. Anyway, I left some water here on your desk—drink it before you come out." Stein stood and walked towards the door.

Lee caught his arm, "How long was I asleep?"

"Two days—drink." Stein closed the door behind him.

Lee downed the glass of water and then dressed himself in the fresh clothing that was left folded at the foot of the bed. The thought that he had slept for two days made him uneasy. He had no idea how far from home they were or whatever happened to his friend, Tholden. He stretched out his sore muscles and stepped out into the corridor.

A small staircase up to the deck was positioned in the middle of the hallway. Both sides of the hall were lined with doorways that Lee could guess were other bunkrooms. All the doors were closed, except for one. He approached it, peered in, and was overcome with a feeling of relief. Garf was asleep, cleanly bandaged with stitching all across his chest. Drogon was sitting in a chair off to the side watching over him. He was reading a massive antique book entitled, *Spell Craft and the Evolution of Magic.*

Drogon looked up, closed the book and stood, greeting Lee with a warm hug, "I'm glad you're okay. For a moment there, I thought we lost you."

"Drogon, Stein told me you saved me—thank you," Lee pressed his face hard into Drogon's chest.

"You're one of us Lee, I would give my last breath to keep you safe," he said.

His eyes swelled, "Thank you. I never had a family like you all. I never felt so cared for."

Drogon knelt down, "You better get used to it. And I'm not surprised Stein already saw you. He has been perched outside the door for days checking in on you. I don't even think he slept."

"He did look tired. He told me not to take risks, but I think I would do it again if I had to," Lee said.

"Of course you would," Drogon laughed, "and if you told him otherwise, he would know you were lying. Stein is easy to get along with for someone like you."

"Someone like me?"

"Yes, someone like you—who has a kind soul, and is true to himself. Stein respects you for that and so do I. I can teach you to be strong, Stein can teach you to be fierce, but no one can teach to have the spirit *you* have. Since you are part of our family now, we can rely on you for things just like this. I do hope you take your own safety more seriously though; we can't do the things you can. We won't be able to bring you back to life."

Lee thought for a moment on Drogon's words, "I will be more careful."

"Good," he smiled.

"Stein said I slept for two days. Are we near Rayton?" Lee asked.

"Donahay claimed to have the entire northern continent under his control, Rayton is part of that. We felt it would be best to head towards the Vian Islands while we think up a plan. Rayton may not be safe after all, and even if it was it wouldn't be for long," Drogon said.

He hesitated before asking, "What about your mother?"

Drogon said, "My brother Duncan is there. I know you haven't met him, but believe me—I'm not worried."

"He must be tough," Lee laughed.

"Oh he is. Maybe you could help me here; why don't you see what you can do for Garf?" Drogon asked.

Lee walked over and held his hands over Garf to read his energy. He could feel the burning of the wounds and the heavy pulsing in his veins. His muscles ached and his blood was racing to mend him. Focusing further, he dipped deeper into his consciousness and caught a glimpse of Garf—he was dreaming. In his dream, he was still fighting the Radiant Empire soldiers, impaled and all. It seemed as though he was winning and overly excited to be in combat. For now, Lee knew there was no more that even magic would do to help him. He could feel it was the slow digestion of seed of life that was keeping him alive. It would take time, and a bit of luck. He would have to heal before the seed passed through his system.

Drogon stood next to him, "What do you think?"

Lee hung his head, "There's nothing else we can do for now, but he's fighting."

Drogon picked up his book and sat down, "I think you're right. You are very impressive for your age. I have known lifetime clerics that couldn't read a patient like you just did. Keep training yourself and someday you could be the best," he lifted his feet to the rest them on the bed, "I found a library in the captain's quarters, there might be something there for you."

Lee skimmed the cover, "Is that where you found that one?"

"Actually no, this one I bought in the Radiant City after we encountered Donahay in Sundale. It cost me most of our gold for this relic," Drogon said.

Stein's voice carried from the doorway as he entered, "Tholden's magic gold you mean."

Drogon laughed, "Of course, how forgetful of me. This book is nearly as old as the Radiant Empire itself and was written by Donahay."

"Who is Donahay?" Lee asked.

"That's right; we haven't had a chance to tell you anything about him." Drogon leaned forward and rested his elbows on his knees, "the story goes that Donahay was an ordinary sorcerer, like Tholden, about two thousand years ago. He always thought himself worthy of being a god –"

"Also like Tholden," Stein added.

Drogon continued, "- even before he could cast a simple fireball. He made it his life mission to enter the heavens and therefore, prove himself worthy of the gods' blessings and power. Unfortunately, this was no simple task. He would have to become the greatest and most masterful sorcerer of all time in order to do this. He spent decades studying, but he was growing older. Realizing he would grow old and die before he could realize his goal, he then shifted his ambition towards extending his life. Even though he originally had simple magical abilities, like Tholden; he was dedicated and somehow managed to do it."

"Unlike Tholden," Stein said.

Lee giggled, "But that doesn't make sense. How could a human become immortal?"

Stein shrugged.

"That's what we want to find out so we can undo it. Somehow, he found a way," Drogon answered. "*Spell Craft and the Evolution of Magic* is the last book he had ever written. You see, some wizards study the ability to prolong their lives, but none have become immortal. You have to understand, wizards and sorcerers collaborate to grow their abilities. That means that if Donahay wasn't sharing his own craft, the magical community wouldn't share anything with him. After this book, he had the ability to cease aging, so he stopped writing—he stopped sharing. He didn't need the other 'lesser' mages, as he considered them. This is an impossibly rare *copy* of the original, which has been lost to time. I can only hope, somewhere in these pages, it has a hint to whatever secrets preserve him."

"Could we use it? Could we become immortal?" Lee asked.

Drogon shook his head, "We wouldn't if we could. Whatever Donahay did, the very nature of it tore a hole in the void itself and unleashed creatures into our world. It took centuries for our peoples to recover. We lost so much life and even more history. That's why there really is no record of our land before the Radiant Empire existed. In all honesty, we have no idea what really happened to Donahay two thousand years ago."

Lee's face showed his confusion, "I never heard that. What kind of creatures? And wait—how did you defeat him in Sundale?"

Stein sighed, "He surrendered when we killed his dominated hydra. And we brought him right to the magestry, just like he planned we would. My plan was to kill him, but I was outvoted."

"Your plan is always to *kill him*." said Drogon.

Suddenly, there was a quick patter followed by the heavy stomps of hooves on the deck above.

"Lee, stay here." Drogon and Stein, said simultaneously.

Lee nodded and sat down on the bed as the others left the room in a rush. After they had cleared the hall and climbed to the deck, Lee got up and stealthily followed to watch from the stairs. As he peered out, he was hit by a gust of stale, dry air. While he had never been to Vian Islands, it already felt like a desert.

When Stein and Drogon arrived on deck, they saw Marlow dashing about, making wide swings with his axe at a blindingly fast figure in fitted green leather armor. She dodged, stepping around him in quick circles with ease. Marlow's inability to strike a blow only made him more frenzied with his attacks as he splintered barrels and railings on the deck with his axe. On her back was a quiver of arrows and a bow that she was making no attempt to grab. It became clear that whoever this elf was, she was not interested in a fight.

"Marlow, enough!" Drogon shouted.

Marlow slashed with his axe, again only slicing through the air. "Stowaway from storage – she climbed up through a porthole," another cleave and another miss, "I'll throw her pieces off."

Stein looked on, amused by the frenzied attacks, "We stole this ship, Marlow, for all we know it belonged to her."

"More reason to kill her," Marlow said.

She finally switched to an aggressive stance with a spin on her heel. The elf ducked below the next axe-swing and keeled back to plant her boot firmly under Marlow's chin. He toppled back and caught himself on the rail, pausing a moment to catch his breath.

She reached up and tied her long, red hair back behind her pointed ears. She then stood and looked over the group as if reading their strength, "I was onboard before you stole this ship," she said softly. Her voice carried a sweet tone and her words were said deliberately. It was clear common tongue was not her first language, "This is not my ship and I don't wish to continue to fight you," she gleamed at Marlow, "if that's what you call this."

He snarled and stepped forward again, but Drogon was already standing between them.

"It's all right Marlow. Who are you?" Drogon asked.

Her green eyes met his, "I'm Gwynn of the **Asra Clan**, I am—I was heading to Vian with a group of dwarves. We should have been there by now, but I see the dwarves never made it aboard."

"No, they didn't," Marlow added.

Drogon approached her, "Tristian was attacked, our group had to make a quick escape and the *Yoshi* was there. We aren't your enemy, I assure you. Right now, we are circling the **Spiral Currents** and haven't routed a course just yet."

"Thank you," she replied, "your words are much better received than a clumsy axe." She reached out to shake his hand.

His hand met hers, "You're pretty quick. Where did you learn to move like that?"

"My clan takes great pride in our ability to defeat our enemies without firing an arrow. It is called **vorsolas**—using your enemies' movement against them," she explained.

"It is an impressive style," Drogon studied her quiver, "and I could see why your clan would want to preserve shot with imbued arrows like that."

"You have keen senses, dragonkin. Yes, each of my arrows does harness an essence of magic. It is part of what my people call **isorin**, being a well-rounded warrior."

"I sense radiant, fire, lightning – yes I'd say you're ready for anything," he paused, "we haven't decided where we are going, but we are only a few hours from one of the larger Vian coasts, Luray. We can take you there and resupply ourselves."

"Thank you, Drogon," she approached the bow of the ship and took a seat by the rail.

Drogon turned towards Stein and Marlow, "We have a problem."

"Let me kill her," urged Marlow.

"What? No—she isn't the problem. At least not right now," Drogon continued, "I'm talking about Donahay. If he has already taken the capital as he claimed, and everything as far as Tristian, then there isn't much we can do by ourselves."

"We'd need an army," Stein agreed.

Drogon nodded, "Yes, but an army that could stop the Radiant Empire is bigger than any one country. It took all three of the **Vian Kingdoms** to defend against the empire invasion in the past. We would need even more swords to stop this."

Stein thought for a moment, "We could meet with King Connero in Vian and ask him for support. He would love the idea of stopping the Radiant Empire. Prime Minister Francesco of **Luray** is an old acquaintance, and smart enough to recognize a threat."

"Old friend? Don't the Vian people and empire hate each other?" Marlow said.

"I said *acquaintance*. We may have been at war at one time, but we kept things humane and spoke respectfully. When the war ended, we began trading. Francesco and I would meet to discuss routes and port authorities," Stein explained.

"I see—then it's a start," Drogon said, "after all, it is closest to the empire and will be the first place Donahay invades."

"What about the elf?" Marlow asked.

"I think it's good she's with us, we could always use a bow," Drogon said.

Marlow growled in protest.

"It's fine, Marlow, don't let her get to you," Drogon said with a hand on his shoulder.

"To Luray, then." Stein ascended the helm and began to steer the course.

Drogon and Lee followed Stein up as Marlow found a crate to sit and stare at Gwynn from a distance.

"Interesting, she knew my name already," Drogon said.

"Maybe she overheard it?" he replied, "She was hiding below deck for two days, who knows what she heard us talking about."

"Maybe, I suppose that's possible. I don't think she's out to kill us, but I think she has some kind of plan. Would you mind spending some time with her to figure out her intentions?" Drogon said.

"I agree," Stein responded. He then looked around to ensure no one else was in earshot. "Of course I can do that, but what if I don't like her intentions?"

"We can decide that when we have more information." Drogon replied.

As Lee joined them, his face was bright with excitement, "She was so fast!"

Drogon laughed, "Weren't you supposed to stay below deck?"

Lee's eyes widened, "I did, but I heard—footsteps and running and wanted to make sure you were okay."

Stein smiled, "Next time, don't follow so closely unless you fix your boot. The sole rubs whenever you step and gives you away."

"You—you knew I followed you?" Lee questioned.

"Dragging that old boot around, anyone would have heard you. We'll pick you up some new ones in Luray." Stein rustled Lee's hair. "You'll be sneaky before you know it."

Lee stood with his arms crossed, "I'll be *so* sneaky."

"I'm sure you will."

"Really—I will." Lee glared.

"Of course."

Drogon began to head back down and his eyes became saddened, as if he remembered something terrible, "Come down when you can, and grab Marlow. There's something we need to do before we make port."

"What is it?" Stein asked.

"Grekk, we need to lay him to rest."

Lee was silent.

"We'll be right there," Stein replied.

The group gathered on deck, leaving only Gwynn at the bow looking on. Drogon exited the quarters carrying the wrapped body of Grekk. He pried up a splintered board and rested the body upon it, tying a cannonball to his feet.

Drogon slid them towards the ledge, stood back, hung his head a moment and began to speak, "We have lost an ally and a friend. A friend who taught me something I'll never forget—how to hope. And now, when we say our goodbyes, I have hope for him. I hope wherever Grekk is now, he knows we live in his name. I hope he is at peace and rests knowing he has done the world great service throughout his life—that he has truly made the world a better place. He lived for the hope of peace, as do I. May **Solihart** guide his light." Drogon kept his head down, "Would you like to say something, Marlow?"

Marlow knelt down to touch Grekk's head. "Grekk was my first friend. He was nice to me when I first arrived in the empire, a time when others left me to hunger. He didn't care I was Minotaur," his large eyes began to tear; "he met his death with honor and died as a true warrior. **Tauros** will guide him to his next great battle where he will fight and slay—gloriously."

Stein nodded, "Rest in peace, Grekk."

Lee reached out to hold Stein's hand, "I didn't know Grekk long, but I know he was kind. I guess if I could tell him something it would be that I was glad to have met him—and that I was sorry," he began to sob. "I'm so sorry I couldn't save you!"

Stein hugged him.

Drogon wiped the tears from his eyes and knelt down. He inched the ball forward until its weight tugged Greek and the plank off the deck. It met the water with a splash and Grekk sank below the surface. They watched as he rippled beneath the waves, becoming more and more obscured until at last they were left staring off into the endless depths of the sea.

A hearty gust filled the sail and the ship was lifted, skimming the surface of the wake. As the sun slipped down below the horizon, the two moons illuminated the coast of Luray. The city grew larger and the sounds of life carried over the gentle slap of the water. It would have been a welcoming site to any seafarer, but for the party it spelled the next challenge. They knew that to overcome decades of war and tension would be no easy feat, but the threat was too great. For any chance of stopping Donahay, they would need all the Vian Forces—and more.

Lee stood with Stein at the helm as he steered the ship into port. The hull groaned lazily as it came to a stop with a bump against the dock. Lee turned to him, "What are we going to find here, Stein?"

"Right now," he said, "we find rest. Tomorrow we will do what we can to make friends of old enemies."

"What if you ask for help, but they won't give it to us?"

"They're not helping *us*. They're helping themselves by joining our cause. I'll find a way to convince them of that." said Stein.

"And if they still won't?" Lee asked.

"Then I'll stop asking and tell them. There is no scenario where we leave here without their help. Luray is the most important future-ally of all, for several reasons. More simply put, I will conquer this country before we leave here empty handed." Stein said with a cold stare over the city.

IX

The City of Luray

*"The mind of one whom is worthy does not perceive
any impossible challenge. It does instead develop
unstoppable solutions."*
Shimmering Mind – A Tribute to Rishara.

The port of Luray was swarming with the ships
of merchants and tradesmen. If not for the smaller size
of the *Yoshi*, the group may not have been able to make
port at all. It was so crowded that larger vessels were
forced to anchor off shore and row their goods in.

There was a steady dry breeze that carried fine,
gritty sand—which stung at Lee's eyes and skin. He
rubbed at his arms at face and could see Stein and
Gwynn doing the same. Drogon and Marlow seemed
not to notice, protected by their scaled and fur hides.
Lee was fascinated by the merchants—the dragonkin,
the reptilian, wrapped completely in clothing, and a
strange cat-like race he had never seen before. There
were some that appeared as a humanoid tiger and others
with the spots of a cheetah. He saw another with the
shimmering black coat of a panther and many more.

"What are those?" Lee asked, pointing at a
person of the cat-like race.

151

"**Katasha**," Stein responded, "don't talk to any of them, understand?"

"Why?"

"They are—dishonest. Most are thieves or bandits and the few that are honest tend to be jewelers and artists, which still—we don't need," Stein explained.

"I don't think that's something you should be telling him," Gwynn said. "You're teaching him to distrust katasha simply because you don't like them."

"I have nothing against katasha as a race, but we are in Luray. Most of the katasha here live in underground hideouts as criminals," Stein responded.

"Do what you want, he's your son," said Gwynn.

Lee wasn't sure why, but he became excited at the thought of Stein as his father. He felt that if Gwynn believed it, then it would be true to everyone else. He waited to see if Stein would correct her.

"I will teach him what he needs to know," he responded.

Lee's face lit up. "Thank you."

Stein smiled.

Drogon moved closer to them, "I think you three should cover up a bit. This sand will blister your whole body if you aren't careful."

"That's a good idea. It hurts," Lee said.

"Actually Lee, I was hoping you'd stay on the ship with Marlow and I," said Drogon. "I want to teach you how to manipulate a healing spell. That okay with you, Stein?"

"Sure," he replied, "we are only as strong as our cleric after all."

"That would be great; I've always wanted to learn how to do that. I can't wait! I'm going to learn to put fingers back on—we need to find someone with severed fingers," Lee said.

"Or we can just sever someone's fingers," said Drogon, "why do you think Marlow is staying with us?"

Marlow wore a frightful look of concern and clenched his grip, "No."

"I'm joking, Marlow," Drogon winked to Lee, "Or am I?"

"Not funny," Marlow whined.

Gwynn pulled out green strips of cloth from the pack behind her quiver and began to wind wrappings around her forearms. Her vibrant elven skin was quickly turning pink from the pelting of the desert sands. She finished and turned to Stein, "I'd like to go meet Francesco with you, Stein."

"Why?" he asked.

"I do not want to stay here in Luray—I was trying to get to Vian. Perhaps, if I help you, you will agree to take me the rest of the way? It isn't far by ship, but if I am left here it will take me weeks to find passage," she replied.

"So? That's not our pr-" Stein said. He looked to Drogon who was nodding with disapproval. "Actually, maybe we could use you while Garf is resting up. We are traveling to all of the Vian territories. It would be a small price to pay for your help, if that's okay with you?"

Gwynn moved towards the docks, "When you are ready, Prince Stein."

They finished covering up by wrapping themselves in dwarven cloaks from below deck and departed. Lee stood on deck, waving goodbye until Gwynn and Stein were out of sight. They made their way off of the *Yoshi* and began pushing through the crowds on the docks. It was impossible to move without brushing against someone and they both kept a tight grip on their coin purse. The jabbering of the masses was so loud, if they wanted to hear each other, they would have to yell. They chose to remain silent and moved on.

As they left the docks, the mob was even more rambunctious with a man yelling, "Sale, best price anywhere," repeatedly. They remained silent as they maneuvered through small streets, vendors selling everything one could imagine, especially jewelry and precious stones. It seemed that Luray was filled with precious gems and it was marketed in abundance.

Stein led them onward, having visited here before; he was familiar with the layout. The city of the clay huts and improvised street additions created a sloppy network of mazelike avenues where most foreigners wouldn't know their way around. Their appearance as outsiders brought stares from the pickpockets and thieves. However, for travelers as formidable looking as Stein or Gwynn, it took only a stare to discourage any would-be criminals.

After about an hour walking through the city, they arrived at the **Luray Capitol Building**. It was a sandstone palace that was surrounded by a short iron fence. A dozen lightly armored guards patrolled the area, but the building was open to anyone.

A dragonkin guard in leather armor approached. He was equipped with only a dulled scimitar and held out his hand before them. "Well met; what is your business here at the capitol building?"

Stein looked him up and down, "We're here to meet with Francesco, but what is your job here?"

"I am a palace guard. I am guarding the palace. Was that not apparent?" The guard waited and received no answer, "Do you have an appointment?"

"You hardly look it. In fact, this hardly appears guarded at all. I'm surprised you even noticed us before we were in the Prime Ministers chamber," Stein said sarcastically, then sighed, "No, we don't have an appointment, but if you tell him Prince Stein is here— I'm sure he will see me at once."

"Prince Stein! My apologies, I didn't recognize you at first with the – scars. Come with me your highness, I will take you to him at once," the guard bowed.

The guard led them across the courtyard and into the building. Inside, he gestured they should wait in a lobby while he continued to the next room. Though Stein and Gwynn weren't thrilled to be left waiting, they were happy to be out of the sun and abrasive winds. A few minutes later, a reptilian servant entered with a silver tray. He offered them water in glass goblets and an unusual assortment of jerky and sweetmeats.

By the time the guard had returned, the pair had enough time to shake the sand from their clothes and cool off. He signaled them to proceed through large double door sat the end of the lobby. They were massive and with skillfully detailed engravings of katasha in fighting stances.

When Stein and Gwynn entered the chamber beyond the doors, a lilting voice greeted them from across the room. They looked up to behold a katasha with the skin of a tiger in brown leather armor. The armor was fitted to the lean muscle of his body and although he carried no weapon, he radiated power. He was twirling a goblet in manicured fingertips. His accent carried the words softly as if it was sung, "Royalty from the Radiant Empire, come to pay a visit to me?"

"Yes, it is good to see you Francesco," Stein and Francesco clasped hands with a heavy thud and held it in a tightening, challenging grip. Stein locked eyes with a smirk, "Your grip is soft. You have been spending too much time behind your desk."

Francesco grinned back, "I prefer these times when I might wield a pen over wielding a sword, Prince Stein. And who is this beautiful woman with you— although clearly—she is not *with* you."

Francesco took Gwynn's hand and leaned forward to kiss it, "I am Francesco. What is your name, *mekora*?"

"My name is Gwynn, I am of the Asra Clan to the west," she replied, "It is my pleasure to meet you."

He kissed her again, "No, the pleasure is all mine. I don't wish to make such presumptions as I did earlier; are you—together?"

Gwynn blushed, "I am traveling with Stein and his companions. We are not romantic."

"I am very pleased to hear, though I could tell a woman as striking as you wouldn't be one to settle," he caressed her hand softly, and stood back, "may I offer you both some water? Or some wine?"

"Wine, please," replied Gwynn.

"Same," said Stein.

Francesco moved to a large curio cabinet behind his desk, pulled a key from his sash, and opened the display with a fluid grace. He picked up a bottle of an illuminated purple wine, as well as three crystal goblets, and set them on the desk. As he poured wine in the goblets, he turned to Gwynn, "You are familiar with **sucrape**?"

"No," Gwynn responded.

"Then you have given me another great pleasure, mekora. Sucrape is a desert plant here in Luray. That is how you pronounce it in my native tongue of **ketash**. In common tongue, it more plainly means purple grape. This plant only exists here in my lands and makes the finest wine in the entire world. It is known simply as sucrape," he handed each a goblet of shimmering purple liquid.

Gwynn stared into the goblet. "This purple is more vibrant than an ostrich blossom. It is beautiful." She took a sip and felt the smooth, sweet taste awaken her senses. There was a relaxing and revitalizing sensation that tingled every inch of her body. Her knees became loose and automatically sat back in the chair, savoring the taste, "this is incredible."

Stein took a single sip and appreciated the sensation before swallowing, "King Treyalt used to joke about how sucrape alone was reason enough to invade."

"Why do you think we fought so fiercely? We were defending it." Francesco laughed as he took a seat across from them, "and thank you, mekora, we take great pride in our wines, especially that of sucrape. For a bottle to sell for ten thousand gold pieces, we seek perfection."

Gwynn's eyes shot open, "ten thousand?"

"Don't worry, for you it is my treat," he added.

They each sat in quiet contemplation of the exquisite wine for a few moments.

"What is mekora?" Gwynn asked.

"It is ketash. It means beautiful one, though in common it would translate to 'my love'. I apologize; I don't frequently have guests from abroad to mind my tongue," Francesco added, "I don't mean to spoil our meet, but there's something I must ask. If you came to Luray for sucrape alone, you wouldn't be the first, but I doubt you came to see me without a reason, yes?"

"You're right about that," Stein said, "I'll be straightforward with you. The Radiant Empire has been overtaken and is currently amassing an army. We believe they plan to invade the Vian territories and then expand throughout the world. Luray or Vian would be the first step in any invasion tactic. We are looking for forces to unify neighboring nations and stop this from happening. In the process, I wish to take back my kingdom and retain our peace."

Francesco was silent for a moment before speaking, "You really know how to break news to someone, Prince Stein."

"For the time, I am no prince. I have no kingdom," he replied softly.

"Let me ask you, who has overthrown King Treyalt?" said Francesco.

Gwynn leaned forward and inched to the edge of her seat, "They are being led by Donahay."

Francesco closed his eyes as if searching a library in his mind. They shot open in shock and affixed to Stein, "The demigod sorcerer?"

"Yes," Stein kept calm on the surface, but anger filled his face with warmth, "he is spreading like a plague and using his magic against my people."

"He has overthrown your father?" he asked. "Unbelievable."

Stein leaned closer, "Donahay has him and most of the Radiant Empire under a spell—a control of their minds. Will you fight with us? You are our first stop, but more nations will join the cause."

Francesco sat back and swirled his sucrape, thinking. He spoke, "This is no small thing you ask of me, Stein. You are asking me to go to war, during a time of peace, and attack an enemy larger than myself."

Stein began to raise his voice, "The war has already started, I assure you. It may not yet have reached your shores, but when it does, it will be the entire strength of the empire. It will be my people killing and dying, against their will. You won't be able to stop an army that marches without fear, without mercy. We need to stop them before this goes further—we need to stop Donahay."

"I believe you, Stein, but you should understand that Luray is not a nation of soldiers. I'm quite sure a man like you would have noticed that on the way through town. We alone don't have the manpower or weapons to stop Donahay if he has the gathered the strength you speak of. I can appreciate the passion you feel for your people, I share it with you—truly, I do. I am sorry, but I won't sacrifice my people," he replied.

Stein rose to his feet, "your people will meet the same fate if you do nothing."

Francesco also stood and did not flinch, "Until there is a more immediate presence that threatens my people, I will not send them to battle."

"Then at least they'll die at home," Stein mocked.

A crackling tension filled the air as the two stared at each other, daring the other to speak.

"Prime Minister Francesco," Gwynn said softly, "this is going to be a war that engulfs the entire world—in one way or another. Our only hope of not becoming mindless puppets to Donahay is to stand and fight together. Stein isn't asking you to march against them alone—to do that would be suicide. What we need is for you to mobilize and ready your troops, build ships, and forge weapons here at home. We need you to be ready because when we have enough nations to fight at our side, we need you to strike with us."

"Most eloquent, mekora," Francesco replied, "Please forgive my reservation; you must understand that Stein and I—the Radiant Empire and Luray have a history. I am familiar with what an obsessive monster like Donahay is capable of, and what he would do to sit among the heavens. In many ways, I appreciate you bringing this warning to me. I suppose if he has already overthrown your father, then there is little that can be done to avoid what happens next," he took the last long sip of his sucrape. "Very well, but there are a few things I desire, as well."

"What do you want?" Stein asked.

"Lower your tariffs on all of our trade agreements throughout Luray," he said.

"Fine," Stein agreed.

"And Gwynn," Francesco said, "dinner here at my estate when this is all behind us?"

"I would love to," she smiled.

"Then I will begin preparations at once, but Stein you must know something. If you don't bring an army that makes me believe victory is possible, I will not march with you. Do not come months from now with a handful of mercenaries and expect me to fight this battle alone. I would then prefer my people 'die at home' as you so eloquently said."

Stein crossed the room to open the door. "I understand. We will send allies here as we travel, so be ready for some tourists."

"I will be here to greet them, but there is one last thing I must ask of you, Stein."

Stein stopped in his tracks but didn't turn to face him, "I'm sure there is."

"On your way back to port you will pass a cathedral to **Rishara** that is barred to my people. We have staged it to appear as renovations, but in reality, I have ordered it sealed off because of a **ghoul** living in the catacombs beneath. I want you to remove it," Francesco bargained.

"No, do it yourself or send your soldiers," Stein said, "we are not running errands for you, too."

"You have given me a greater task that requires my attention. As I said before, Luray is not a nation of soldiers. If I send my guard, there will be losses, and every capable arm is invaluable, don't you agree? I would need time to better train them, where as a ghoul would be no issue for you. Do this, as a token of our alliance. Good faith, if you will."

"We'll do it," Gwynn responded, nudging Stein through the door.

Francesco smiled, "Thank you, mekora. I look forward to our dinner."

Stein and Gwynn left the room, cleared the lobby, and departed the capitol building. As they made their way down the steps, through the field, and began navigating the streets in silence. They could see the tall bell tower of the cathedral rise above to mark the way of their next task. After a brisk walk, they arrived at the **Cathedral to Rishara**. The entryway was roped off and hanging at waist height was a sign that read:

DANGER: Renovations in Progress – *DO NOT ENTER.*

"I guess we can't enter," Gwynn laughed, "we'll have to come back when they're done with these renovations."

Stein held up the rope and gestured forward, "After you."

She ducked under, "For a prince, you're quite a gentleman."

"It's the least I can do," he replied sarcastically, "after all; this is the pointless quest you accepted for us."

She knelt down and began picking at the lock on the door, "Why do you do that? Why do you feel a need to be so standoffish towards anyone who expects something from you?"

Stein positioned himself behind her to hide her from anyone on the street. "You know nothing about me."

"I don't need to *know you* to know you. I know your type," she replied.

"How do you figure?" Stein asked.

"Men, nobility, warriors without equal, you're practically a walking cliché. Let's see, you travel with friends who *ask* of you rather than serve your own kingdom who *demands* of you—probably because you have control issues. You have this compulsion to battle everyone because you are looking for a challenge you never find in a fight. And oh yes, you're last in line for the throne so I bet you didn't get enough attention from your father. That probably explains why you travel with that young cleric, trying to make a relationship that you never had as a child." Gwynn then felt the lock release and pressed the door open, "Got it." She squeezed inside as Stein followed.

The cathedral, from floor to ceiling, was decorated with enormous white marble tiles. Tethered from the rafters thirty feet up hung embroidered tapestries of red and gold. Each one depicted an image of a katasha overcoming enemies and puzzles. They were arranged to tell a story of how, using only a focused and clever wit, one could bring great changes to the world. There was a stillness throughout the cathedral, and an evil odor that made Gwynn and Stein uneasy. They continued up the aisle and between the pews, keeping on guard.

About the seats were scattered articles of clothing and bags. It was clear that people had fled from here in panic. They continued onto find that not all were fortunate enough to escape. Blood and fur was splattered on sections of the floor and chunks of rotting meat were smeared about.

"I need you to know something," Stein said.

"That I was right about you?" Gwynn laughed.

"No, Gwynn—that I've killed people for less than that," he said in a threatening tone.

Gwynn stopped short, "Are you threatening me?"

"Warning you. Don't think you know me, and don't ever speak of Lee as someone to fill a hole in my life," he pressed.

"Look Stein, I didn't mean anything by it. I think it's great that you're taking him in as your own. I can promise you to never bring it up again, but *you*— you don't get to threaten me. Never. In fact next time you do," her eyes locked onto his, "one of us is going to die." She held out her hand and spoke with authority, "Deal?"

Stein smirked with satisfaction and clasped hard, "Deal."

"I can't tell if that's madness in your eyes, or respect," she joked.

"Can't it be both?"

As they stood between the pews, there was a loud thud from behind the altar. Gwynn drew her bow in an instant as Stein approached with hands buried in his pockets. They flanked around the stone to find a large wooden trap door behind it that was the length of a stairway. The plank was pinned down by cathedral relics and statues that were thrown over in haste. Another thud, it was even more powerful this time and shook the weights in place.

"Have you ever killed a ghoul?" Gwynn asked.

"Today will be my first, you?" he replied.

"Same, but you know only one of us can kill it," she grinned.

Stein felt his face twisting to that strange position—the one that Lee sometimes brought out of him and warmed his cheeks, "What's the bet?"

Gwynn was confident, "A thousand gold pieces?"

"You're on."

They began to toss the relics and figures from the door, working to be faster than the other. Then, there was another movement from below. Whatever was barred beyond the door, kicked it once, and scurried deeper into the catacombs. The two eagerly lifted the door to expose a grey stone staircase leading down into darkness. On the inside of the door were deep claw marks that had created small punctures and splintered the boards.

Gwynn looked closely at the marks. "It's not much larger than us."

"It doesn't matter how big it is," Stein said.

"You're right, but it's good to know what you're up against," she said. "Look at this; it was already scratching its way through. It's a good thing we came before it made its way out."

"Let's get this done quick. We don't know how long we have until Donahay is on the move. We have many more places to go before we're ready," said Stein.

Stein held out his hands before him and summoned his long crooked scythe, igniting it in a bright flame. He led the way down, illuminated by the glow of his blade. Gwynn followed close behind and peered past his shoulder with an arrow notched and ready. They continued downward, alert and confident; fixed on *who* would slay the creature. There was a faint snarling that echoed back up the stairwell. It beckoned them deeper and deeper into the catacombs. Nearer and nearer towards the flesh eating monster thought to be a ghoul and through a thickening smog of rot and death.

M.C. Grimm

<u>Into the Catacombs</u>

"Over time a weapon will dull, but you must always wield a sharpened wit."
Shimmering Mind – A Tribute to Rishara.

It reeked of decay in the damp halls. The stone floor had a shallow layer of stagnant liquids. Every step was met with a splash that further soiled their clothes. On either side were open indentations cut into the stone where coffins were stacked between shelves and displayed with plaques. Most of the coffins were broken open, leaving the corpses either mutilated or missing entirely. Stein and Gwynn descended the walkway, side by side, led by the light of the burning scythe.

"It smells like the ghoul has made home down in these catacombs for a while now. It's rancid down here," Gwynn said.

"They're never pleasant, but this is different. Normally, you aren't stepping through chunks of rotting meat," Stein exhaled, "this ghoul has definitely been down here for a while."

"Luckily I can't see the floor, so I'll pretend you didn't just tell me about that 'chunks of meat' part. You spend a lot of time in places like this?" She asked.

Stein slowed his pace. "Dungeons and battlefields, but they aren't much different from this—death in the air, and blood on the ground."

Gwynn looked at him, "That doesn't sound like much of a life, Stein. I mean, what do you do when you're not killing things?"

"I thought you already knew everything about me," he mocked.

"No, I know your type, but I don't mind getting to know *you*," she said softly. "You don't have to be so mysterious. It's okay to let people in."

Stein opened one of the undisturbed coffins. All the flesh had decayed and all that remained was a skeleton in formal dress. "It must track by scent. It didn't need to break this one open to know there was no food inside."

"That's good to know," Gwynn dismissed him. "I know you have two brothers, are you close with them?"

"You're not going to stop until I tell you something, are you?" he asked.

Gwynn smiled.

"I was close with Victus," Stein explained, "he and I used to spar together during training, we are very competitive people. We pushed each other, maybe even sometimes a little too hard. But, he was the heir to the throne and I was trained to fight his battles—protect him at any cost. When our father sent him on a mission, I was his personal guard. We spent a lot of time together."

"That actually sounds really nice, like you two were inseparable," she said. "Where is he now?"

"I'm not sure. I guess Donahay has him under mind control back in the Radiant Empire. Drogon saw him outside of Tristian when the soldiers attacked them. He said Victus didn't look like he was physically hurt, at least."

Gwynn nearly whispered, "I'm sorry, Stein. That's an impossible situation. I'm sure you'd do anything to free him, wouldn't you?"

"Almost anything," Stein responded.

"Almost?" She nearly shouted, "I would do anything for my sister, absolutely anything. Don't you love him?"

"I do. But there are some things that are worse than death—worse than loss," he said with confidence. "There are some things that I wouldn't do for the sake of others, even if that meant Victus or I must carry the weight of it. He would say the same thing."

Gwynn shook her head in disagreement. "That's not what love is. You should–" she stopped herself with another thought, "wait, have you ever been in love?"

"He's my brother, of course I–"

She interrupted, "I'm not asking about your brother. Have you ever been *in* love?"

She reached out and grasped his hand from behind. Stein stopped in place, still facing forward down the corridor.

"Have you?" she asked again.

Stein looked to her over his shoulder. He opened his mouth to speak, but was silenced by a snarl from up ahead. He pulled his hand from hers and gripped his scythe.

Gwynn raised her bow and drew back an arrow that shimmered with a red hue.

From the darkness could be heard the rapid splashing of the creatures as it advanced. It went silent for an instant, until at last it entered the dim light. It was midair led with both mangled claws, reaching out towards Stein. Its mottled skin was green and stretched thinly over a disfigured skeleton. There were no eyes, ears, or nose. Just a flat, bald face with empty sockets and elongated fangs.

The ghoul was quick, but so was Stein. The creature's swipes met the blackened shaft of his scythe.

It continued relentlessly, slashing and swiping at him, throwing all of its body weight behind each attack. Stein found himself at a disadvantage in the shallow catacombs with such dim light. With such an extended weapon, when he would parry the creature to counter attack, his blade would catch the ceiling and walls. He was on the defensive.

Gwynn patiently waited behind Stein, moving back and forth, as he evaded and lined up her shot. In an instant where Stein had dodged aside the creature, she let loose the arrow. The red hue erupted the arrowhead into flame to leave a scorched trail dancing in the air. It followed from her fingers, straight into the hollowed eye socket of the ghoul, through its skull, and splattered the wall behind. The arrow embedded itself into the stone, still emitting a low flame.

But the creature didn't flinch.

In the next motion, it pinned Stein to the wall, pushing hard against the shaft of his scythe and making quick bites towards his neck. Stein maneuvered from side to side, barely avoiding the ghoul's gnawing fangs.

"Fire and regular weapons won't work!" Gwynn screamed, her voice echoing in the catacombs.

"Do you have anything else in that quiver?" Stein said as he dodged another vicious bite. Being face to face with the ghoul, he watched as the hole through its skull was slowly shrinking. "It's healing."

Gwynn was concentrating. "Yes, radiant magic would work—of course," she drew an arrow from her quiver that gave off a golden glow and centered herself. With a slow exhale, she released the shot.

At that same moment, Stein escaped from the ghoul's claws. The golden streak of radiant light only grazed the ghoul's back shoulder. It burned and boiled at the flesh, leaving embers that continued to burn away at it. It howled and scratched furiously at its back. When it couldn't reach the wound, it threw its back at the wall and grated itself against the hard stone.

"Again," Stein said.

Gwynn reached back into her quiver, "That is my *only* radiant arrow." She peered down the dark corridor. "I'll have to get it. Can you keep it busy?"

"Seriously," Stein scoffed, "you only carried one?"

"They're expensive and I never miss—you ruined my shot."

Stein laughed, "And you missed! Go get your arrow; I'm going to try something while it's wounded."

Gwynn snatched her fire arrow from the wall. It burned like candlelight as she disappeared down the hallway.

The ghoul was still frantically chaffing his back against the wall. He was moving and pressing so firmly that skin and clumps of blood clung to the stone.

Stein looked on at the creature's torment, "I wonder," he smirked. "If I cut you into enough pieces, will you die?" He stood against the opposite wall, leaned back and held low onto the shaft. The scythe was long enough to reach from wall to wall, but with a twist, he had room for movement. He sliced from left to right in one quick horizontal motion. It cleaved deep into the ghoul's gut. Chords of entrails with thick dark ooze began to seep out. Stein then flipped the blade and carried it back from right to left, slicing just above his first cut. He flipped it again to cut higher, and again— higher. He slashed back and forth, back and forth, more quickly with each swing. The creature teetered as if only the force of each blow was keeping him standing.

At last, Stein let out a soft, maddened laugh with the final arc of his scythe. With that, all the slices of meat and flesh fell to a pile of black ooze on the floor. The head rested atop, slowly sinking in. He stood back, breathing heavily, staring at the pile of ghoul. He was covered in bits of the creature and the black splatter of blood. Every inch of him had some trace amount of its blood, even the bared teeth of his maniacal smile.

Gwynn returned and stepped back into the light of his scythe, holding her bow and the golden arrow. She looked towards Stein, concerned, "are you alright?"

The question took him by surprise. It wasn't until hearing her voice that he could feel the warped look on his face and imagined what it must've looked like. His eyes were wide with bloodlust and fixed on the mutilated ghoul. His mouth twisted in a demonic grin. He relaxed and recomposed himself, "I'm fine, just finishing up here." He felt uncomfortable and embarrassed, but wasn't sure why. He turned back towards the cathedral and slung his scythe over his shoulder, "A thousand gold pieces, right?"

"Hey, Stein?" Gwynn beckoned.

"Yeah?" Stein peered over his shoulder where Gwynn had her bow fixed at the head of the ghoul. The black ooze was reaching out like strings and reassembling bits of the creature. They were layering and filling, one atop the other and taking on a form sprawled out on the ground.

"I just wanted you to see that it is still alive," she smiled and released the arrow.

As the golden streak of light disappeared into the head, a hollow thud resounded through the hall. The movement in the ooze immediately stopped and all the meat began to melt down into a pool of ghoul.

Gwynn stowed her bow on her back and skipped past Stein, "A thousand gold pieces," she chuckled. "You can pay me at the ship."

Stein let out a sigh, "You won, I'll pay."

"And you can't say things like 'you couldn't have done it if I didn't put him into a pile of ghoul' because that wouldn't be very sportsman like," she said.

"You know, I didn't think of that," Stein said, "And now that I think about it, you *did* miss when he was still standing."

"Only because you ruined my shot!" She said.

Stein laughed, "I'm not being serious—I won't say anything like that. You killed it; we'll leave it at that."

They left the catacombs and quickly made way across town and back to the port of Luray. Pushing through the bustling masses, they arrived back at the *Yoshi*. They were greeted with the heavenly smell of someone cooking below deck.

Stein and Gwynn entered the mess hall where Lee, Marlow and Drogon were already sitting to eat.

"Welcome back!" Lee said excitedly.

"They tried to wait for you, Stein, but I was starving," Marlow said.

"It's okay; I know we were gone longer than we should have been," Gwynn said.

"We weren't waiting for you," he snarled.

"No more of that, Marlow," Stein said. "If she is traveling with us, we can make dinner peaceful. I think we can manage that, especially without Tholden around."

Gwynn smiled at him.

Marlow scowled, "Fine."

"How did things go with Francesco?" asked Drogon.

"He had us run some errands for him, but he is going to start preparing for war," Stein said, "he is only going to follow through, however, if we have an army beside us. If not, his forces will stay here to defend Luray."

"I understand his concerns," said Drogon. "We will have to make sure we have a fleet at our side."

Lee tugged at Stein's sleeve, "Drogon taught me how to throw a healing spell from further away."

"That's impressive, good job, Lee. You'll have to show me how you do that," Stein praised, "nicely done, Drogon."

"It helps that he's such a good student and a remarkable cleric. He is already more skilled with healing than I am," Drogon said, "all we need to do is polish a few spots and then we will have to find you a more experienced teacher."

"Thanks Drogon," Lee smiled. "So, can I help when we go to the next place?"

"I want off this boat, too," Marlow said.

Drogon laughed, "Lee, I think you still have a little ways to go before we should put you in harm's way again—don't you think?"

"No," he argued, "I think I'm ready."

"Soon," Stein rustled Lee's hair. "We're near Vian, it's only a couple of hours from here. We should head there tonight while the wind is at our back."

"You're right, but first," Drogon raised his tankard, "there is something I need to share with you all. I meditated on the task we have ahead of us and realized how daunting it truly is. In fact, if I was with any other party, I wouldn't be putting any coin on us making it through. Being completely honest with you, I could think of no better cause than to guard what we have right here at this table. I am honored to call you my friends—and—my family."

They raised up their cups and clashed them together. Before it touched their lips Gwynn asked, "Anything else in this meditation?"

"Grekk, Tholden, Garf," Drogon paused, "the path behind is what lead us here, but the real journey is on the road ahead. Don't over think this, I said what I meant, just be happy and drink with me. There are no other warriors I would prefer at my side when the day to end Donahay soon comes. We will see this through, together."

The tankards clashed again and they celebrated, simply having found one another. Even after dinner, there lingered a sense of unity and family. It was so infectious that they couldn't help but smile at one another while passing in the halls.

Lee brought some food and water in for Garf and repositioned the pillow beneath him. He sat in and read aloud from *The Tales of King Treyalt* in hopes that Garf could hear it. Lee felt the turning of the ship as it left port. He felt the groaning protest of the wooden hull. It complained as if it wasn't yet willing to wake from sleeping in the safety of the dock. Lee leaned back and became lost in thought. Luray had been such an interesting place and the katasha were so different from anything he had seen before. He wondered what strange creatures might be in Vian. Before he realized he was so tired, Lee was lying on the chair next to Garf, thinking of their next adventure. He closed his eyes, his mind wandering.

He saw the flitting of small wings, glistening with a vibrant golden sparkle in the light of a sunset. She turned slowly to face him, a tiny elf woman? No, she was a **nymph** with a lightly tanned skin and wearing a dress made of green scales and leaves, all pinned together with its thorns. She smiled at him playfully.

"Hello," Lee said, "I'm Lee. Who are you?"

Her cheeks blushed red and her entire face was brightened by her smile, "I'm Spring, it is wonderful to meet you, Lee."

Spring's smile was contagious, Lee giggled, "It's wonderful to meet you, Spring. What are you doing here? I am in a ship with my friends. Is this real?"

She flew around him, magic falling as glitter from her wings. She tossed by an emerald colored hair that matched her wings, "What you believe in is what makes anything *real*, don't you think?"

"I mean, kind of, but is this a dream?"

"Yes, of course it's a dream. I couldn't stop to talk for this long if you were awake. Being a dream doesn't make this any less real." she huffed, "In fact, sometimes the things you do in your dreams can inspire you to do great things when you're awake."

"Oh yes!" he said, "I had a dream once that I could throw a ball of energy and just today, my friend Drogon taught me how to do that."

"Yes, just like that," she flipped in the air, "and since you could imagine it, and dream it, you could believe it was possible when you were awake."

"You're right," said Lee, "I wonder what else I could dream into existence."

Spring smiled, "Yes that's exactly it! Never stop believing—dream big, Lee. The goddess, **Mora** has great plans for you."

His eyes widened, "Mora!?"

"I just had to meet her *chosen* while I was passing through." Her eyes fixed onto his, reading him, as she floated at eye level, "Okay, goodnight!"

Lee shot up off the chair with a gasp. He looked around the room, studying every detail through his groggy stare and rapid blinks. After a moment, his eye caught a glimmer on his nose. He traced it with his finger and held it out—a single speck of golden glitter.

XI

<u>A Vian Celebration</u>

"The most fortuitous of men and women cannot hope to resist temptation indefinitely. Eventually, in one form or another, I will have them. They are always seduced by greed, wrath, pride, lust, sloth, gluttony or envy. They will all be mine - in time."
Confessions of the Temptress – A Tribute to Eve.

The *Yoshi* pulled into port and was immediately met by two fairly intoxicated dragonkin guards—one of green scales and the other tan. They helped to tie the party off and boarded the ship. As the guards stumbled up the ramp, the sky was lit up with fireworks. It appeared they were being launched from a small castle at the center of the city. The streets were filled with celebrating crowds. Booths with games of chance and food vendors with exotic smelling offerings were scattered about the city.

Lee stared up at the fireworks in awe.

"What would an empire ship be doing here?" The green-scaled dragonkin asked.

Drogon stepped forward to greet them. "We are here to meet with King Connero; we have very important business with him."

"Important business?" he probed, "What kind of business?"

"Unfortunately, I can only relay that message to the king himself. Will you take me to him?" Drogon said.

The tan dragonkin spoke next, "He's busy, you see, it's his birthday and the city is celebrating tonight. You'll have to wait here until the week's end."

"It can't wait," Drogon insisted, "I assure you that if we don't speak to him immediately there will be consequences."

Both dragonkin approached Drogon, their hands hovering over their weapons.

"Are you threatening us?" asked the green.

Stein and Marlow lowered into a combat stance. The dragonkin grabbed at their sword hilts.

Gwynn came up beside them, "What he means is our message is a matter of national security and it would be your *king* who would deliver the consequences to you for wasting our time getting it to him."

"That is most certainly the case," Drogon agreed, "may you please go tell him that messengers from the empire have arrived with matters of national security and that you have us detained at the docks? We will wait here, as you've asked."

"Alright, alright, don't get all worked up. The castle is up the main road, you can make your own way by yourself. We have to mind the docks and can't leave, you understand. Tell them Eingard sent you up to see the king." He turned to leave the ship, "Come."

Gwynn turned towards Stein and Marlow, "We won't be very well received if we kill the first two people we meet, wouldn't you agree?"

Marlow turned away in a huff.

Stein turned to Gwynn, "This was where you wanted to be, right? What's here for you?"

"I am also here to see King Connero," she answered.

"You never told us that, what for?" he asked.

"No, I didn't," she replied, "why don't we head to Connero now and you can find out."

"Gwynn," Drogon said, "you are welcome to come back to the *Yoshi* when your business is done. I agree we should go see the king at once. I doubt he'll be taking guests late into the night, important or not. Marlow and Lee, look after Garf and the ship."

"I hate being left on the ship," Marlow grumbled, "what do I do with the boy?"

He laughed, "He's a boy, not a **phoenix**—keep yourselves entertained."

As Drogon walked down the ramp and left the ship, Stein and Gwynn followed closely behind.

Marlow looked at Lee, staring at him as if he were studying an alien creature.

"What?" Lee asked, "Why are you staring at me?"

"Nothing, I'm not sure what to do to pass time. Human young are so fragile," he said.

"I'm not a child. Well, let me ask you; what do you like to do for fun?" Lee asked.

Marlow's face showed confusion, "What do you mean?"

Lee was excited, "When people pass time they do things they enjoy. You know things that make them happy. I like to read, I like to play games and dance. I love to dance!"

"Those things are a waste," he said contemptuously.

"Those things are fun," Lee said.

"No, they are not."

"Okay, fine. What do minotaur do for fun?" Lee asked.

"We spar and wrestle. We fight and throw each other down to prove ourselves to Tauros. We make our brood stronger and when there is more time to pass after battle, we rest and prepare for the next," Marlow explained.

"I don't think that's fun either." Lee replied. "Oh, I know something you would like, one of my favorite things in the world—to eat!"

Marlow stomped the deck in agreement, "Better, cleric. That *is* fun."

"There are lots of places here. We should go get food," Lee said.

"Drogon says to stay on the ship."

"Come on, we're hungry. We'll go right there," Lee pointed to a food cart at the end of the docking area, "and then we'll come right back."

Marlow lifted his snout into the air and took two deep sniffs, "Good smells—like candied pork."

"My nose is much smaller than yours, even I can smell that. Let's go see what it *tastes* like." Lee said.

Marlow did not need any more convincing, "Come."

He led them down the ramp onto the dock. There were so many people dancing and stumbling through the streets that the two kept being bumped by happy, inebriated strangers. Lee found the energy contagious and stared in amazement at fire jugglers, sword swallowers, and belly dancers. Many of the intoxicated women seemed to run into Marlow on purpose and try to rub his horns, fascinated by the rare site of a minotaur.

He ignored them and moved directly towards the food vendors, "Stay with me, cleric." Marlow didn't slow down a bit. When someone was in his way, he moved them.

Lee nodded while drifting side to side. He was entranced by a kai musician banging wildly over some drums and cymbals. Lee stood for a moment watching, "You're really good."

The musician gave him a friendly nod and smiled as Lee continued to watch.

He quickly realized Marlow was no longer in front of him, but still leading up the street towards the food shops. Luckily, a minotaur was still very easy to spot in the crowd. Lee gave the musician a final nod before giving chase and once reunited, they finally reached the large tan wagon where the sweet smell was coming from. A flap was pinned open and overhead read *Maxine's Meats: Honey Glazed and Candied Pork's for 2cp.*

A half-breed woman with mossy green skin leaned out, greeting them with a smile and a tilt of her head.

"What can I get for you fine gentlemen?" She offered.

Marlow slapped twelve copper pieces down and turned to Lee. "What do you want?"

"I don't know," said Lee, "isn't honey glazed the same as candied?"

Marlow shrugged and turned back, "Three of each."

She pulled the food from the grill and slipped each one into a sleeve. Then, she handed them to Marlow. "Thank you, handsome."

Marlow handed one of each to Lee as he began gnawing away at the pork.

"This is so good," Lee said, "way better than Tholden's cooking. His stuff always tasted old. Real food is always better than conjured food, I've always said that."

Marlow looked to Lee. "I'm done, finish up. We should go back." While he claimed he was finished, the obvious bits of meat in his teeth could be for a snack later on.

"No wait; we have plenty of time until they get back to the *Yoshi*. Let's go watch a show!" Lee shouted over the rabble.

"A show?" he asked.

"Yeah, I saw them setting something up over here—come on."

Lee grabbed at Marlow's giant hand and began pulling him further up the main street where he saw a crowd gathering. As they approached, they could see a human man in a black top hat standing atop a small-elevated stage. There were all sorts of props scattered about: boxes, swords, cages with owls, tanks with snakes and all colors of ropes.

He just finished a well-practiced bow and looked out over his audience, "Good evening my most beautiful spectators. My name is Oswald; I am an illusionist from Luray and a master of magic. I have been asked by King Connero himself to come to these very streets and perform a special routine for you. Tonight, I will dazzle you with the mysticism of the maker's arts. I will baffle you with feats that are impossible for the weak-minded to understand. Yes, tonight, I will defy the very laws life and death. Are you ready?"

The crowd cheered loudly in anticipation from all around them.

"Are you ready?" he repeated with intensity.

"Yes!" Was roared at the stage.

"Yes!" Lee shouted. "Come on Marlow, I want to be in front." He pulled him forward and pressed through the crowd until Lee was resting his hands on the planks of the stage.

Oswald rolled a contraption to the center of the stage. It appeared as a black cube suspended from four small posts at each corner with chains. Positioned at the base was an arrangement of long swords that were polished and displayed in stands. "For this first feat, I will need a volunteer."

Lee's hand shot up and waved frantically, "Me, please!"

The illusionist looked right past Lee and pointed out an elegantly dressed elven woman. "You, my beautiful lady, please come up."

She held her hand to her chest and hesitated, "Oh no, I couldn't"

"Please, I insist. This will be quick and effortless," he coaxed.

The crowd shifted to allow her up to the stage. She climbed up and looked over the spectators nervously.

"Don't mind them; you'll forget they're even there in a moment. What is your name, my dear?" Oswald asked.

"Leia," she answered.

"Leia is such a fitting name for such a beautiful woman. Would you please come closer?" He brought her over to the black cube and unhinged a latch to open it. Inside, he showed how the cube was a restraint. It had a cut out on the top for a head to stick out, and two holes down below for legs. On each side, there was an opening for the arms. The box also had many slits on each side that were the perfect width of a sword. It appeared to be designed to close around the torso area and hold a person in place while allowing sword's blade to be pierced through. "May you please touch this here and tell our friends what it is made of?"

The elf rubbed her hand along the outside of the box. "It's made of iron."

"Very good, thank you. May you please also touch these swords, and please be mindful of the sharp edge. Are they real weapons?" He asked.

She reached down to touch one of the swords and quickly yelped—pulling her finger to her mouth. She nodded to the crowd and was met with a hearty laugh.

"Oh I'm sorry, but I did warn you," Oswald chuckled, "enlighten our audience. Are they real weapons?"

Leia held up her finger to show blood running down her hand, "They're real."

"And what do you suppose would happen if one of these swords was to be run through my body?" He asked.

She gasped, "You would be killed!"

"Killed?" He looked out over the crowd, "I told you, I am a *master* of magic. It would take more than one sword to kill me. In fact, my dear Leia, how many swords do we have there?"

It took her only a quick look to count them, "Twelve."

"Ah, twelve swords. What do you suppose running twelve swords through me would do?" Oswald said.

"It would certainly kill you!" She said in horror.

"You don't give me enough credit, killing me would take at least thirteen." He turned to face the crowd, "what do you think? Should we try it—twelve swords against a master magician?"

The spectators cheered wildly, caught up in the horror of the moment. The number of people looking on had now grown to fill the entire street. Leia, however, was shaking in place, her eyes wide and a bead of sweat on her forehead.

Oswald approached Leia and leaned forward to kiss her hand, "My dear lady, I could not ask this of you. Thank you so much for taking part. Let us please bring our hands together for Leia."

The applause guided Leia off stage and back to her partner.

"Now," Oswald continued. "I need another volunteer. This person must be brave and strong stomached. He or she must not be faint of heart. Is there any such man or woman out there?"

Lee again raised his hand and began to jump up and down frantically, "Me, pick me!"

Oswald scanned over the crowd until his eyes fell upon Lee, "Alright youngling, but are you sure you have what it takes?"

"Yes, I do!" Lee replied.

Oswald grinned, "Then come on up. Please let us have a round of applause for our next assistant."

Lee turned to climb the steps, but Marlow caught his arm.

"Be quick," he said.

Lee gave him a hasty nod and then ran up to the stage to greet Oswald with a handshake.

Oswald silenced the crowd, "Brave youngling, what is your name?"

"Lee Cheng."

"Lee Cheng? That is hardly the name of a brave warrior. Are you sure you have the stomach to run twelve swords through me?" he asked.

"Yes!" Lee shouted, "And I'm a cleric too, so after I stab you twelve times, I can help you so you don't die."

The onlookers laughed and even Marlow snarled with excitement.

Oswald positioned himself inside the cube and reached his arms out through the holes to close it around him. He slid the latch into place and looked out over the crowd. "I call this, *The Twelfth Chest*. Lee, you may begin when you are ready, but it is imperative that you run all twelve swords through me. Don't stop, no matter what—do you understand?"

Lee nodded, "Yeah, sure, but why?"

"Why?" he scoffed, "because I promised our fans that I would take twelve swords for them! If I die at ten... just keep going!"

Lee picked up the first sword and looked around at the massive amount of people that had now gathered. They stared up at him with excitement, holding their breath for him to stab the box. Marlow looked to him and nodded hastily, flicking his eyes back towards the ship, anxious to leave.

He pushed the sword through the box as Oswald squirmed and groaned. The cold steel of the blade grinded on the edge of the metal box, inch by inch. Lee then felt the blade pierce the meaty contents of the box and, with resistance—slice through.

Lee could recognize real pain from stabbings and deep wounds—this looked more like discomfort. Lee wasn't convinced. He picked up another two swords and stabbed quickly into the box.

Oswald let out a shriek as sweat dripped from his forehead, "Look at you, two at once? I picked a good assistant if you are enjoying this."

The crowd let out a laugh—all except for Leia, who fainted.

Lee picked up another sword, and another. He kept driving them into the box, playfully and with eagerness. Six, seven—Oswald cried out. Eight, nine, ten—he yelped and squirmed. On eleven, he collapsed limply within the box. The people went silent. Lee held the twelfth sword and slowly pushed it through. As soon as the hilt met the box, Oswald's head shot back up and his arms straight out.

He gasped sharply, "I live!"

There was a thunder of applause as Oswald reached in front of him and unhinged the box to swing it open. He revealed all twelve swords stuck into his torso from different angles. With a twist and a shake— he snapped the blades from his body and stepped out of the box with ease. There were tears to his clothing, but no blood from a wound. The crowd cheered in bewilderment.

Oswald bowed to the audience and faced Lee, "You have been such a remarkable assistant; would you help me with one last trick?"

Lee looked back at Marlow who was shaking his head from side to side with disapproval. Lee replied, "I'm sorry, but I have to go meet my friends."

"Oh, but this trick is special for *you*. In fact, if you don't help me, I would have to wrap up my show right now and not continue. What do you think ladies and gentlemen, should he help or should we all go home?" Oswald asked the crowd.

There was a wave of unfriendly disapproval from the audience—evident by booing and pleading for him to continue.

"Come on, kid." a woman pleaded.

"Just go with it!" ordered another.

Lee smiled, "Okay, okay, I'll help. What's the trick?"

"It's simple in theory, but terrifying in nature. In fact, if a lesser illusionist were to attempt it – things could go horribly wrong," he panned over the crowd, "I am going to turn this boy invisible. You heard me right; I am going to use my powers to make this boy disappear. He will still be here, able to knock over my stool or topple my hat, but you will not see him."

"Excuse me, Mr. Oswald? You said things could go horribly wrong?" Lee asked with concern.

"That's right, Lee. Sometimes this spell might in fact banish you to another realm. Other times you may turn invisible and never able to be seen again. Alas, those things don't need to concern you. You are in my well-practiced hands and I will see it through young one. Come and lay down right here."

Oswald whipped off a cloth covering to what appeared to be an altar. It was ornately decorated with engravings of a longhaired woman, sparsely clothed and shown in different settings. In one, she appeared as a shadow watching over a village. In another, she was playing a game of cards while in a third rolling a crude depiction of dice. Lee had trained in different religious rites in the name of his clerical training and recognized this woman. Her name was **Eve**—the **dark-elf** goddess of deceit, treachery, and gambling. Though it was common for traveling magicians and tavern goers to worship Eve, it was more typical of those lacking ability. Her followers were more likely to pray for a slight of trickery rather than a hand of luck.

Lee looked towards the frustrated Marlow and shrugged. He then approached the altar and laid flat on his back.

Oswald stood over him and held out his hands, "Watch me closely as this trick will be my finale—I only have enough magic in me to do it but once. I will now make this young boy invisible to the untrained eye," Oswald waved in the air and orange sparks began to rain down on Lee and the altar. Lee coughed as they began to erupt into a thick smoke. The crowd was silent, staring on. Oswald leaned in to whisper, "Give my regards to the Axeman."

Suddenly, he felt the altar beneath him give way and he was free-falling, gagging on the smoke with tears in his eyes. He fell only a short distance and landed on a something soft, but boney. He must have dropped below the stage, because he could hear the muffled cheering of the crowd, as Oswald was moving about the stage overhead. He was claiming Lee was moving different items trying communicate. Lee was too focused on catching his breath to feel disappointed in the fraud.

He tried to dry his eyes to see, but he was immediately lifted from the ground by two men. Each of them lifted him up under an arm having already shoved a gag into his mouth. Lee was dazed and struggled with all his might, but these two men were as big as Drogon, and he still felt like he was suffocating. As his feet kicked viciously at the air, his eyes cleared to see the strangled corpse of an overfed magician to be what had broken his fall. At the sight, Lee became frantic. Twisting his body, he threw himself about and managed to hook one of his feet on a rafter above. He held on for his life as he felt the two men pull harder; stretching his body until finally - he slipped. He twirled in place and managed to get one arm loose.

"This one is going to be trouble," one of the men said.

"Knock him out," the other ordered.

Before Lee could free his other arm, a heavy thud met the back of his head. He fell forward and hit the ground with a crash. His cheek scraped the dirt as his mind raced in terror. He tried to push himself back up, but his body wouldn't move. He coughed up the gag while gasping for air.

"Look, now he's all bloody. The boss isn't gonna like that," one said.

"You told me to hit him!" said the other.

"Not that hard," the first one leaned over him, "actually, maybe you didn't hit him quite hard enough. He's still got some fight in him."

Lee heard their voices through a soft ringing in his ears. He saw a blurred shadow crouched over him. But he watched helplessly, as that blurred shadow raised hits arm back, clenched a fist, and thrust it into Lee's face.

 XII

Of Love and Treachery

*"May the weary rest and the wounded heal, so as we
may once again return home and to those we love."*
A Generous Life – A Tribute to Mora

Allegiances with King Connero were established with ease, he was eager for a reason to once again battle the Radiant Empire. But the long walk up and down from the castle to the dock that was made even more time consuming by the vendors and street performers. Drogon picked through small trinkets at the shop, while Gwynn watched the acrobats. Stein felt guilty not allowing Lee to leave the ship and explore the celebration. He wanted to bring him back something from one of the many sellers and at last, after much searching, he found something worthwhile. After only a few hours, Stein, Gwynn, and Drogon returned to the *Yoshi*.

"Lee, I have something for you." Stein called out, opening the sack in his hands.

The ship was silent.

"Lee? Marlow?" He called again.

Drogon made a round through the cabins and came back on deck, "It's only Garf down there. They aren't onboard. They must have gone ashore for something," he laughed, "that kid of yours, Stein."

Stein looked out over the festival, searching the crowds. His eyes filled with concern.

Gwynn rested her hand on his shoulder, "I'm sure they're fine, probably just went to play a game."

"I'm sure you're right," he replied.

While it wasn't a very late hour, the bands stopped playing and packed up while the rabble in the streets began to clear out. Vendors were forced to close up their carts and shops and everyone was directed back to their homes. The group looked out over the city in confusion. Finally, Stein spotted Marlow. He was limping from a large wound on his leg, his hands bound behind his back, and being led towards the *Yoshi* by several dragonkin guards—a group that included the two from earlier.

Stein dropped the sack to the ground. A small pair of brown leather boots fell across the planks. He leapt down to the dock and made his way towards Marlow. Gwynn and Drogon followed close behind.

Eingard shouted before Stein had a chance to speak, "No! You need to get back on your ship. The festival is over, and no one is allowed in the streets. You may not leave port until the investigation is over.

If you try to leave, you will be considered a primary suspect and will be pursued by the **Vian Armada**."

"Where is Lee?" Stein said.

"Who?" he asked.

"A magician did something to him," Marlow answered. "Oswald. He took him and wouldn't tell me what he did with him."

"We hear you, bull-face," one of the guards joked, "still doesn't mean you start tossing the man around and tearing apart his stage over a magic trick."

Marlow shouted, "That's exactly what that means!"

"That's enough," said Drogon. "Release him; we will take him onboard with us. Is the festival being shut down to search for Lee?"

"I don't know *who* Lee is," Eingard said. "The entire city is on lockdown until Queen Sana is located. We believe she has been kidnapped this evening and we will be searching every inch of Vian until we find her." He cut Marlow's bindings loose and tossed his axe to the ground near Drogon. "Get on your ship and stay there until we sort this out."

The group gathered on the dock and watched the guards disperse. They were out in force and moving everyone out of the streets.

"What happened, Marlow?" Stein said.

"The kid wanted food so I took him to the festival. He wanted to see a magician. Oswald invited him on the stage for a trick. I waited until the end of the show and asked where Lee was. Oswald said he wasn't the guy who knew. So, I asked him again—harder—this time. He said he really didn't know. So, I kept asking him until the guards started attacking me. They were taking me to a cell when the queen went missing. They said a wooden note turned up at the palace."

"It was a wooden note?" Gwynn asked.

"That's what they said," he nodded.

"What did it say?" Drogon said.

"They didn't say."

Stein began pacing the dock, "We should start off at that stage and get to Oswald. From there we," he stopped short, staring at the hull of the ship. A single discolored plank was attached to the *Yoshi* and held in place with a hatchet. Stein reached out to grab it, read it, and threw it to the ground, "A wooden note."

The group looked down on the plank. Crudely engraved on the board were the words:

Crew of the Yoshi; come to the north ridge by sunrise. Duel for the fate of your kid. Well played, Gwynn – Axeman.

Stein summoned his scythe and stepped towards Gwynn, the shaft gripped tightly in his hand "What do you know about this?"

She looked up at him. "Stein, I didn't have a choice," her voice was shaking, but she didn't not move away.

"You had no business with Connero, so why did you come here, Gwynn? Tell me what you know *now!*" Stein demanded.

Drogon moved to stand between them, "Hold on Stein, give her a chance to speak."

"While you still have air in your lungs—*speak!*" Stein's voice roared.

Her eyes swelled, "He has Porbella! Stein, he has my sister."

Drogon turned to face her, "Who is *he*?"

"The Axeman. I don't know his actual name, but that is what he calls himself," she peered past Drogon and into the furious eyes of Stein, "you have to believe me, I didn't want any of this, but I need your help. He's a duelist and a warrior without equal. He travels the world looking for his greatest challenger, but instead leaves behind a trail of death. He took Porbella to get to my father, the leader of the Asra Clan. My father was sick and passed away before we even had the note, but the Axeman doesn't care about that. Please Stein, I came here so that I can end this and free my sister. I told you I would do anything for her, but he is rumored to have traded his soul to be impossibly strong and I know that I can't beat him. If you duel him, you might win - you defeated a reaper."

"What does he mean by 'well played'?" Drogon asked.

A single tear rolled down her cheek, "I tried to barter for my sister. He said that if my father wouldn't come than it would have to be someone even more formidable and mentioned your name Stein. He heard about Sundale and how your group took down the hydra."

"Why Stein?" Drogon said.

"I knew about Sundale and the reaper; I mentioned your name. You need to believe me; I had no idea he would do anything to Lee to lure you in, like he did my father. I was going to ask for your help," Gwynn pushed past Drogon and stood before Stein. The flame was radiating off his scythe and rippling her hair. The heat dried the tears from her face. Her eyes gleamed, "I promise you, I would never put Lee in danger. Stein, I would never want you to feel the pain I have felt since my sister was taken. I love her, as you love Lee. Please, help me—help me stop this monster."

The intensity of his stare could have burned a hole through a weaker person, but Stein dissipated his scythe and kept his eyes fixed onto hers. "You manipulated us."

"I'm so sorry." Her eyes met the ground.

His voice trailed, "You manipulated *me*."

"I—not all of it." She reached out her hand.

Stein turned away. "I will get Lee back, and your sister. When it's done, you will leave and make sure to never cross my path again."

She nodded, "I... understand."

Stein looked to the group, "Then we go to the north ridge, and kill the Axeman."

"He didn't do this alone." Marlow said, "We kill them all."

Drogon was reading Stein's face, "Brother, we have to be objective. There is too much at stake and remember how daunting the force behind us is. Lee and Porbella are our main goal here; we can't risk their safety out of anger. You can't run in blindly and unleash your emotions. If we push them into a corner, they may get desperate. We need to focus on getting them out in one piece before anything else."

"They have to die," Stein said with a cold stare.

"You're focused on the wrong people," Drogon explained, "*they* have to live. Lee and Porbella—have—to live."

"They will," Gwynn said, "we won't let anything happen to them."

Stein took off at a sprint, maneuvering through the shifting crowds and making his way towards a darkened alley. Drogon and Gwynn followed as Marlow limped behind. His eyes were fixed on the glow of the north ridge. The light of the two moons traced its outline across the horizon and several fires danced at the top—faintly visible from this distance. At every cross street to the alley, he stopped to let Drogon peer around the corner for guards, never once losing his focus on that far ridge. At this pace they would definitely make it before sunrise.

For Stein, every second felt like days. He was breathing heavily, his muscles burned, and every beat of his heart pushed him to move even faster. He was consumed entirely by his wrath and he held no mercy for whomever they were going to find at the top that ridge. His face twisted with rage as he mumbled, "I'm coming for you."

To be continued...

M.C. Grimm

The Tome of Insights

The world of **Radiant Heroes** is another realm of fantasy where only the wildest minds dare to wander. Here, many humanoid species, gods, and magic cover the lands. You will find bold words from the story further defined here in this **glossary**. There are also some hints at what is to come in future Radiant Hero works.

Amon– A shapeless and primordial evil that predates most other gods, Amon originated from the shadow created by the spark of existence. His essence is said to live on in the void and in acts of malice and wickedness. Though many of his texts have been destroyed over time, the original tomes are known only as *The Black Book*.

Amorous Day- A day recognizing the importance of love, passions, and family that is inspired by the cosmic-love of *Luna, the Moon Goddess* and her *Starshine*.

Antidote Potion - This green potion can counteract venoms and poisons, both natural and crafted, throughout the land of Radiant Heroes. While a lesser antidote would be ineffective against a more advanced poison, most adventurers find a minor antidote sufficient to handle most poisonings during through their travels. Comes in varying strengths; minor (pale green), major (olive green), and super (dark green).

Asra Clan– An elven clan nestled in the southern wilds of the Radiant Empire. Independent and self-sustaining, the clan has preserved its traditional lifestyle for unknown generations. Gwynn has stated to be from this clan.

Bow– A ranged weapon for shooting arrows that is typically made from a curved wood with a tightly drawn string.

Cattletail Rose – A long-stemmed and elegant flower that comes in a variety of colors. It is gifted to show love or affection due to its beauty. The color of the flowers is dependent on region of growth. Therefore, there are some colors of the cattletail that will likely not be seen in other areas of the world due to import costs.

Clan Unkle– An Orc clan that is led by Simone Unkle and makes camp in the southern wilds of the Radiant Empire. Garf has stated to be from this clan.

Cleric- An individual who is capable of performing healing magic and rituals.

Cocoon Silk – Silk from cocoons of creatures undergoing metamorphosis. It is most often used when dried.

Common Tongue– Is universally spoken throughout most of the continents of the known world.

Though every sentient being has the physical ability to speak it and at least a basic understanding of the language, some remote and isolated tribes may be the exception to the rule.

Commons, The – The southern blocks of Tristian are built for more functional and practical uses and are therefore more affordable. They are inhabited by the working class.

Cookies - You needed to look up cookies?

Cotton Wheat– A fast growing crop that sprouts buds stuffed with cotton. It is the one of the most popular crops due to the ease of its farming and demand of its harvest. There is a saying among farmers, "When in doubt, plant yourself some cotton wheat." What did you expect? They are simple farmers.

Crowlastte– In the days of old, a kai god was driven to madness by the death of his kin and became restless, vengeful and murderous. His name was Crowlastte and he became an agent of chaos, igniting sparks of conflicts simply to watch turmoil unfold. The supporters of his madness follow a text known as *The Chill of Death*.

Crystal Palace– Also known as the Radiant Castle, this elaborate crystal palace is decorated with the most precious gems and metals available. It is residence to the King of the Radiant Empire and his family.

Dark-Elf– Also known as a *gray*, a dark-elf is a cousin to the elf. During the earlier years of the elf species, some took to live in caves while other moved into the forests. Those that remained in the caves became known as the grays. They share the abilities of a heightened dexterity and reflex. A dark-elf has skin of a varying gray shade and a keen sight in darkness. They are sensitive to sunlight, but it is not lethal to them.

Deathrobe– A mythical robe worn by a reaper that is tattered, torn, and comes only in black. Not much is known of the abilities possessed by the robe.

Deathscythe– A scythe that is wielded by a reaper. It is crafted from the magic of the spirit realm and sealed by the cold touch of death (The Grimm or leader of reapers) itself. Every deathscythe possesses frightening abilities and each harnesses a single element. (i.e. Stein controls fire.) A deathscythe will dissipate to ash if its wielder is defeated, therefore it can't be claimed from a reaper. It can however, being a magical entity; change allegiances to another wielder.

Dinsley Clinic- Clinic in Tristian where Master Mulag practices the healing arts.

Djinn– Also known as a Genie, djinn are magical beings that feed off the essence of other magical beings. Many djinn bind themselves through pacts with powerful sorcerers, completing tasks in exchange for some of their essence. This relationship typically lasts until the djinn have become more powerful than the mage. At which time, they consume the being entirely rather than simply parting ways. Why then might a mage make a pact? Djinn are cunning and loyal for the time in which they are bound – making them a fierce ally. They are also the only known creatures, other than *the maker*, that possess creation magic (a.k.a. the ability to make something from nothing).

Dragon Tongue– Also referred to as Draconic. This language was derived from that of dragons and passed down by many races said to descend from them. Though some races are incapable of creating the pitches necessary to speak fluently, one can be trained to understand it. Some creatures (i.e. Dragons) only speak in Dragon Tongue.

Dragonkin– Believed to be descended from the bloodline of dragons. Dragonkin are a powerful species in tuned with natural magic. They are taller and broader than the average humanoid with an armored-like scaly hide, the snout of a dragon, and the fangs to match. This species is made up of many colors, but most are red, green, or tan. Though many have long pointed tails like the reptilian, some are born without. Dragonkin are as warm-blooded as the dwarves and though they can survive in any climate, they favor more dry and arid conditions. (i.e. Drogon)

Dragonling– This is a name given to two different creatures. The first dragonling is a newborn (recently hatched) dragon that has yet to develop its ability for flight or reach its toddler size. The second is a descendant of the dragon, one that remains a small size its entire life. This dragonling never grows much larger than a hawk and tends to travel in groups for protection. Some adventurers train dragonling for sending messages and scouting. (i.e. Argon)

Dwarf– Stout and sturdy, the dwarven peoples are proud and ancient race. Both males and females are short in stature with broad builds that favor heavy weapons due to their natural strength. Dwarves are resistant to colder climates and dislike tropical regions. This is credited to their stocky build and high metabolism resulting in above average body temperature and a consistent need for hydration. Dwarves do not tend to have magical abilities. (i.e. Nor.)

Eel Wheat– A fast growing crop that is meant to harvest after the storm season. Eel wheat grows off the light of the sun *and* the static of lightning. After the crop has been charged by a storm, harvest is performed, and the buds can be ground to a charged dust. It is no longer in the form of lightning energy because the plant has metabolized it. The process results in energy charged dust present in a raw and easily manipulated form. *Eel wheat essence* (charged ground dust) is the base ingredient in a majority of potions.

Elf– The oldest species to walk the lands is that of the elves. Tall and lean, an elf is naturally agile with a keen insight into magic. Any skill that requires finesse and dexterity comes easily to them. Their above-average life span is nearly five times longer than that of a human. This allows them to dedicate time towards mastering many skills before even reaching adulthood. (i.e. Gwynn)

Elven Tongue– One of the oldest languages in the world, Elven is credited as the first language not made by nature or the gods. If one has the physical ability to speak common, they may learn elven.

Fornesio– The eastern island of the Vian Kingdoms.

Gardener Park– A well-manicured park and playground located in northern Tristian.

Gashimar– The most massive continent of the known world, Gashimar consists mainly of forests and wilds. It is inhabited by the greatest number of wild races and creatures that lurk within the woodlands and swamp covering the land. Gashimar politically is separated into factions and clans. The most powerful 50 citizens are ranked in strength and possess political control over the clans. Only by achieving rank through dueling may one achieve the title of Padrino, the ruler of Gashimar. Upon becoming the ruler, one would relinquish their name until death and take on the title of Padrino. A duel for the title of Padrino must be to the death. Marlow stated to be born here.

Gaweed– A hallucinogenic herb that was native to Gashimar, but has since been cultivated throughout the known world. Gaweed is outlawed in many areas because it has limited alternative uses.

Great Axe– A double-headed axe that is used as a large and heavy weapon. Specialized training and strength are necessary to use this weapon effectively.

Eve– The reptilian goddess of deceit, treachery, and gambling. Many of her followers regard her as 'lady luck' due to the influence of her will over chance. She revels in lust and greed. Those who seek her good fortune and follow her faith have scribed *Confessions of the Temptress* from their personal experiences with the will of the temptress herself.

Half-breed– Every sentient race is capable of mating with another. When a dissimilar pair conceives—the child is known as a half-breed. In the majority of cases, the offspring takes on the appearance of the mother's species and shows no evidence to the heritage of the father. In other cases, they take on the build of one with traits of another. (i.e. Garf)

Harryman's Herb– Owned and operated by Lester Harryman out of Premiere. Harryman's Herb caters to the finest ingredients of herbs and spices that any food or clerical establishment could have need of.

Healing Potion - By combining aged *heartbane, eel wheat essence* and boiled water one can create a healing potion. One of the most consumed and demanded potions, the healing potion has the ability to mend minor wounds and requires to skill to use. While this potion (also known as a crimson) is always recommended to be ingested (helps fight infections from open wounds), it may also be poured directly onto the injury. Comes in varying strengths based on the charge of the *eel wheat essence*; minor, major, and super (very rare).

Heartbane – A durable herb that grows in a wide variety of climates and conditions. It is a base ingredient used in many healing rituals and potions.

Hosridon— The dwarven god of adventure, travel and voyages. Hosridon was one of the first gods created and, for his love of pioneering, was tasked with mapping out all existence within a tome to share with the other gods. When he had finished his work, he set the book aflame and stated that the complete secrets within it belonged only to The Maker. When the other gods attempted to kill him for his disrespect, Hosridon became impervious to their attacks – credited to The Maker's blessing. Those embarking on great journeys and travels often seek the blessing of Hosridon. His followers created *Claiming the Heavens* to share his story.

Human– A common species that is found on every continent. Known for being adaptable to every terrain and climate, humans are regarded as enduring and diverse. Height and weight vary throughout regions based on diet, exercise and upbringing. Though the human body possesses no true natural advantages over other races, they are able to take on nearly any art. (i.e. Lavi, Lee, Tholden, and Lester)

Hydra - A large, many headed, snake like monster said to possess blood with some of the world's most poisonous tendencies. While hydra are rare to encounter in the wild, they are more commonly summoned under the control of powerful wizards to defend strategic locations.

Hyriel– The elven god of life and nature who was first to plant seeds across the barren dirt of the world after its creation. Followers of his faith worship nature in all of its forms and his instructions for a collaboration of living are chronicled in *Circular Harmony*.

Isorin– The elven term associated with being a well-rounded warrior. This would describe someone familiar with multiple fighting styles, proficient with many weapons, or studying multiple magical arts.

Kai – A cousin to humans, kai are of a similar build and appearance. The only identifying difference is the natural formation of tattoo-like markings on their bodies that is present from birth. It is said by the eldest kai that these natural markings are the written destiny of the kai who bears them – deciphered only by the wearer. Kai have similar adaptability and abilities to human with a greater natural affinity towards the magical arts. (i.e. Stein, Victus, Vulcan)

Katasha – Speed and agility exceeding that of even the elves, katasha are regarded as the swiftest species in the world. They possess a humanoid build with the fur, claws, and head, like that of a predatory feline. There are variations of this breed scattered through the land and all are regarded as katasha. They may appear as a leopard, cheetah, panther, lion, or tiger. (i.e. Prime Minister Francesco)

Ketash– The language of the katasha. It is difficult, but not impossible, for a non-katasha to speak due to the subtle purring used to pronounce certain letters of the language. *Mekora* - My love. *Sucrape* - Purple grape.

Korthus– The orc god of war and conquest. His tales of glory and savage battle are documented in *The Flail of Korthus*. It is the war cry to orc barbarians everywhere.

Luna, the Moon Goddess- Luna, the most captivating celestial body, is a source of healing and nurturing energies. Also known as the *Green Eyed Moon*, it is said that she was born from the wishes and dreams of a drifting star known as her *Starshine,* who sought true love in the heavens. From this cosmic union of a fulfilled destiny was born two smaller stars. This family orbits one another in a heart-shaped pattern, creating the constellation-worthy happening frequently admired by lovers and dreamers alike on *Amorous Day*.

Luray– The western island of the Vian Kingdoms, Luray was originally led by a Prime

Minister—an elected official. During the times of the great war from the Radiant Empire expansion, the Prime Minister was never removed from power. At the time, it was considered an issue of national security and the transition of power would create too much instability. Upon his death, the title and role were passed down to his son, Francesco. Present-day, Francesco remains as ruler over Luray with the title of Prime Minister, but the authority of a king.

Luray Capitol Building– This building is frequently mistaken for a palace due to the additions and renovations that have been added on by the acting Prime Minister. Though he lives within the structure, Francesco reminds his people that this is a Capitol Building, and the lower floor is open to the public for all political concerns.

Magestry, The– A specialized and enchanted magical prison designed to indefinitely hold the most capable master sorcerers and wizards. Although these places are only rumored to exist, and known by many different names, it is believed that there is one in almost every nation.

Magic-Weapons- Some magic weapons and equipment have names. This is the name given at 'birth' (being forged and imbued with magic) by the enchanter or smith. The name will follow the weapon for as long as it exists and will only be revealed to the ones deemed worthy *by* the weapon to wield it. By learning the weapons name, one may unlock its abilities.

Maker, The– The spirit and power by which all gods, worlds, life and existence has come to be. Though none have any true image of its being, the essence of magic and creation is credited to The Maker - both by gods and lesser creatures.

Minos- The language of Minotaur. Pronounces with a serious of low growls and snarls to syllables. Words are often drawn out giving each word an emphasized meaning to determine the intent of each word and therefore the sentence. You will notice a Minotaur speaking *common* sounds broken when it is actually direct translations without the emphasis on driving syllables. *Toren*- One who fights because they are broken.

Minotaur – Minotaur are large, powerful, and aggressive humanoid creatures possessing the fur, hind hooves, and head of a bull. Most are incredibly territorial and do not communicate with outsiders. The more civilized Minotaur live in isolated villages exclusively with their own kind and attack intruders at will. It is extremely rare to encounter one outside of its community unless it is pillaging or part of a band of mercenaries. (i.e. Marlow)

Mondook - An extremely poisonous orange berry that grows on a particular vine in dense, isolated woodland. It is rare. Mondook berries are utilized in the crafting of the most common and lethal poisons available throughout the world.

Mora– The elf goddess of mercy, selflessness and healing. It is said her image has appeared to those in need and has shown her to have eyes of gold. The followers of her faith teach the text *A Generous Life* which is followed by every practicing cleric throughout the land.

Northern Villas– The northern blocks of Tristian are well kept and constructed by some of the most brilliant engineers of the time. These estates are afforded only by the wealthiest families in the city.

Nymph- Sometimes referred to as a fairy, a nymph is a small, winged, elf-like creature, possessing of natural magic and a sensitivity to people and their true alignment.

Orc – Rivaling the Minotaur for strength, but exceeding them in ferocity are the orc. Although they are not as large, they are still above average in size and weight. They are green or tan-skinned with a wide framed muscular build. Orc live in tribes and tend to be very aggressive towards outsiders. Since they typically have violent raider-like and man-eating tendencies, they tend to be able to make home in the less civilized areas of the world.

Padrino– The most powerful individual citizen, deemed ruler of Gashimar.

Path of Rubies– The most prestigious and sculpted residential street in Tristian.

Phoenix Dust – When a phoenix transcends and turns to ash, some ash may be preserved without disturbing the creature's resurrection. This ingredient is required for some of the most masterful rituals and potions. Phoenix dust is the rarest ingredient in alchemy since the phoenix lives throughout a hundred years cycle and typically transcends in isolation. It is, by far, the most expensive magic ingredient.

Pike– A long pole topped with a spearhead and with a double-sided axe blade below. This weapon is frequently used by supporting infantry.

Premiere– The residents of the Northern Villas demand only the most exotic of goods. Premiere is the market of northern Tristian that satisfies that demand.

Quiver– A container or carrier for arrows/bolts. It is frequently fastened to a sling worn on the back, but can be attached to the bow, leg, etc.

Radiant Capital, The– Home to the royal family and capital of the Radiant Empire. The center of the capital is the Crystal Palace along with the most exclusive high-end markets and tradesmen.

Radiant Empire, The– The largest and most powerful kingdom throughout the land. It is ruled as a monarchy that has sought to unify many parts of the world through military conquest and economic manipulation in the past. Stein was born a prince to this kingdom.

Rayne– The long sword carried by Drogon. Its properties include radiant and healing magic. Rayne has displayed its loyalty and faithfulness to Drogon which allows him to tap into its abilities.

Rayton– A moderately sized fishing town located off the coast of the continental Radiant Empire. Drogon claimed to have family there.

Rishara– The katasha goddess of cleverness and cunning. She is praised for her wisdom of life and tactics in combat. Rishara is given recognition for providing innovation and refined skills to lesser creatures, allowing such industrialization as turning grapes into wine. Those who seek wisdom ultimately seek her favor and follow her teachings in *A Shimmering Mind*.

Reptilian – A common race in the wilder parts of the world, reptilian are also known as lizard-men and scalers. There are many breeds and colors depending on the region of origin, but all are of average height and are covered with a scaled hide. Being one of the few races that is cold blooded, reptilian tend to avoid colder climates as they very quickly feel its degenerating effects. This species is most naturally-resistant to diseases and poisons. (i.e. Grekk)

Scythe– A tool made for harvesting, normally a long wooden pole that is topped with an extended curved blade. A scythe is also rumored to be used by reapers who 'harvest' the living and escort them into death.

Seed of Life– A high level and extremely complicated recipe that has resurrection capable qualities when combined with healing magic. When prepared correctly, the seed will restore life to any creature that has been killed within 24 hours. If not created correctly, it may have no effect or extreme side effects. These side effects include, but are not limited to: blindness, coma, development of new allergies, paralysis, loss of vocal ability, fear of plants, cannibalism, facial numbness, psychosis etc.

Senate House of Fornesio- The nine senate members of Fornesio that act as one of the two parties of government in addition to the Duke. The Senate deals with civil matters, commerce, and all non-military budgeting. Stein refers to them as *the house of petty debate.*

Shadowbane – Also known as *lights kiss* or *sun wisp*, shadowbane is used to suppress the effects of dark magic and curses. For less powerful curses, shadowbane is capable of curing the disease completely. Some adventurers will consume it prior to embarking on a journey where there is known dark magic involved. Doing so will act as a preventative.

Sky Sparks– A rare ingredient of alchemy. It can only be harnessed by someone with magical abilities by containing the natural energy of a lightning bolt.

Solihart– Solihart was a brave dragonkin knight who battled the darkness of evil during the formation of the world. He was immortalized by the maker as a god and inspires courage, honor and ferocity in combat while remaining true to his cause. His followers, typically of paladin training, follow the doctrine of *The Wayward Warrior*.

Spiral Currents– All the currents of the seas meet just south of the Vian Kingdoms. These harsh conditions have protected their southern shores from invasion. Due to the vicious nature of the spiral currents, very few ships in the world are designed to withstand travel through it.

Star Serpent– A mythical creature of the cosmos that is rumored to survive on the light given off by stars while swimming through the sky. Not much is known about these creatures since they have never come down from the night sky.

Sucrape— A desert grape that only grows throughout the Vian Territories. The grape has rare flavors and possesses the ideal qualities to make wine. Because of its limited growing ability and supply, sucrape and the wine made from it is an exotic and expensive commodity.

Sundale– A small manufacturing town located within the Radiant Empire. The party claims to have defeated a hydra there recently.

Tauros– The legendary Minotaur warrior who was said to save of the last of their species from extermination at the hands of would-be 'heroes'. He inspired the formation of minotaur clans and instructed what each could contribute towards strengthening the brood. Tauros is believed to have been deemed worthy and given god-hood for his feats of might. The Minotaur people have no written texts in his honor – it is their belief that the roar of valiant battle is his true tribute.

Tristian– A large trading city located on the outskirts of the Radiant Empire. The port of Tristian is used for all imports and exports to the Vian Kingdoms as well as northern Gashimar. Lavi and Lee are believed to be from this city. Episode 1 begins here.

Vampire– Fabled creatures of the night, vampires require the blood of mortal beings in order to survive. They are natural predators with increased strength and agility. This is further enhanced with age and frequency of feedings. A vampire can't survive in sunlight and is susceptible to a variety of radiant magic. Due to the prior facts, vampires tend to be of a pale complexion (if applicable) and reside far from religious buildings and holy ground.

Vetala– Ghastly spirits that are capable of possessing cadavers. They are born by unnatural and evil acts of the living and develop power by possessing bodies and spreading their curse. The possession is generally limited to the dead, except in the case of a vetala lord or alpha.

Vetala Lord– (i.e. Vulcan) Also known as an Alpha. The vetala lord is a vetala who's power has become so developed within a being that it is self-sustaining and no longer able to swap hosts. It is powerful enough to be capable of spreading its curse even unto the living. Those that are susceptible to the curse are ones corrupted by greed and power while or those having a disregard for others. These corrupted are not all inhabited by the Alpha, and so they are not vetala. Instead they become corrupted, seemingly ordinary and unchanged, but submissive to the curse and will of the Vetala Lord and taking on some physical traits at will.

Vetaless– A female vetala. For unknown reason, females that are overcome by the curse of the vetala lord can be afflicted with incredible strength and reflexes vs. males which typically become corrupted. The vetaless senses are heightened to rival that of the Alpha, however they are still submissive to its will.

Vian– The northern island of the Vian Kingdoms, Vian is ruler by King Connero and is largely inhabited by dragonkin and reptilian. It is the most militaristic of the Vian territories and provided the greatest resistance against the Radiant Empires expansion.

Vian Kingdoms, The– Three large, allied, island nations that remain independently ruled: Luray, Vian, and Fornesio. Originally operating as separate entities, the three kingdoms created a binding alliance to hold against the Radiant Empire's advancing military threat.

Void, The– Known by many names: the afterlife, spirit realm, the between, unknown, abyss, limbo, neutral plane, etc. Not much is yet revealed to this plane of existence, but it is believed to be a place where only the dead and gods can travel freely.

Vorsolas– An elven fighting style created by the Asra Clan. A primarily defensive style that favors utilizing the movements of an attacker to gain an advantageous position for retaliation.

West Gate, The– The final un-ruined section to the original wall that once fortified Luray from the invasion of the Radiant Empire.

Yoshi– A small, dwarven trading ship that the party acquired in the port of Tristian. It is able to traverse through many sea conditions at an average speed and has no noteworthy combat abilities as it possessed only a single cannon.

And more to come!

<u>About the Author</u>

M.C. Grimm is a born and raised New Yorker living in Wallkill. He takes on the day-to-day adventure of survival with a blissful optimism and found his soulmate to be the moon.

www.ingramcontent.com/pod-product-compliance
Lightning Source LLC
Chambersburg PA
CBHW051242250626
47155CB00009B/3138